Burning Secrets

Jane Blythe

Bear Spots Publications
Melbourne Australia

bearspotspublications@gmail.com

Paperback
ISBN: 0-6484033-5-1
ISBN-13: 978-0-6484033-5-7

Cover designed by QDesigns

I'd like to thank everyone who played a part in bringing this story to life. Particularly my mom who is always there to share her thoughts and opinions with me. My awesome cover designer, Amy, who whips up covers for me so quickly and who patiently makes every change I ask for, and there are usually lots of them! And my lovely editor Mitzi Carroll, and proofreader Marisa Nichols, for all their encouragement and for all the hard work they put into polishing my work.

OCTOBER 28TH

Silence could be the loudest—and most frightening—sound there was.

It was full of unknowns, and the more time you spent in it, the louder it got.

She carefully eased open the back door and crept inside.

It squeaked a little as she pushed it closed behind her, and she froze. Her ears strained for any signs that someone had heard her. If she was found sneaking into the house in the middle of the night, her life would be over.

Several seconds ticked by and nothing.

No footsteps sounded, no lights switched on, no one appeared.

She was safe.

For now, at least, but tackling the stairs was going to be a lot harder; the house was old, and those things creaked if you looked at them wrong.

Step by painstakingly slow step, she crossed the kitchen, then began the even slower climb up the stairs. This wasn't the first time she'd done this, so she knew which steps were the noisiest, and where the best place was to put her foot on each one to avoid the creaks and groans.

There was always the temptation to rush, but this was a case of slow and steady wins the race. It took close to ten minutes, but finally, she had made it all the way upstairs and into her bedroom. She closed the door, then leaned back against it and sighed in relief.

The longer she kept sneaking out after everyone else went to bed, the higher the chances that she would eventually get caught. Was that going to stop her? No way. If it was the only way she could get what she wanted, then she was going to keep doing it.

Besides, she kind of liked the adrenalin rush.

She liked to live life on the edge; it excited her, and she hated to be bored. Excitement was the spice of life, and she liked her life very spicy. Taking risks was as common to her as breathing; the bigger the risk, the better. Her mind was constantly spinning thinking up new ideas, new ways to push the envelope. Sooner or later she'd end up crashing and burning, but why worry today about something that wouldn't happen until tomorrow?

It was her motto for life.

If she wasn't scheming or plotting, then she may as well be dead.

Smirking to herself, she tiptoed to the en suite. She might be in the safety of her bedroom, but there were still several people in the house, and any one of them might be awake and hear her walking about. Her family was a nosy bunch, and if someone heard her up and about, they were likely to come and find out why.

She brushed her teeth, shimmied out of her clothes—leaving them where they fell—then stepped into her favorite pair of pajamas and ran a brush through her hair. On her way to bed, she paused to run a hand over her Halloween costume. There was only ever one person she went as, a character who was just like her, the Queen of Hearts from Alice in Wonderland. She'd loved the over-the-top, irrational, unreasonable queen and her off-with-their heads mentality ever since she could remember. When she was little, and all her friends were playing Disney princesses, she always gravitated toward the villains. Why be the good girl when you could be the bad guy? Bad guys always had so much more fun.

A giant yawn nearly split her head in two. She needed to sleep.

Leaving the costume hanging on the closet door, she went and climbed into bed and snuggled under the covers. Although it was nearly November, the weather was still warm during the day. It was only when the sun set and night came that you knew winter was just around the corner.

Her eyes were just starting to fall closed when she heard something that nudged her out of her half-asleep haze.

What was that?

It sounded like glass shattering.

Was someone else up and about tonight?

That was her first thought, and her second was how much had they seen? Not everything she did was something that she wanted to be public knowledge. In fact, most of what she did wasn't something that she wanted to be public knowledge. She was about to get up and see who'd been snooping on her personal business when she both heard another sound and saw something.

Her irritation was quickly replaced by fear.

The sound was a crackling noise, and there was an orangey red glow outside her window.

Fire.

Was the house on fire?

The house was on fire.

On *fire!*

She was dreaming.

Yes.

That was it.

That had to be it.

Touching her fingers to her arm, she pinched herself as hard as she could, and yelped at the accompanying sting of pain.

She wasn't asleep.

Maybe she was just imagining the sound of the flames.

Yes.

Yes.

Imagining things.

She did have an overactive imagination, as anyone who knew her would attest to.

On badly shaking legs, she wobbled her way from the bed to the window.

When she looked out, her brain still didn't want to believe what it was seeing.

There were flames everywhere, and they were rapidly claiming more of the house with every second that ticked by.

She was going to die.

She was going to die.

She was going to die.

Her brain was stuck on that one thought. It couldn't process anything else. It couldn't try to move. It couldn't formulate a plan. It could barely remember to breathe.

Breathe.

It wasn't until that moment that she realized the room was already filling with smoke.

The fire shouldn't be spreading this quickly, should it?

What did that mean?

"Eeeee!" she keened aloud. She was losing it. Burned alive was a horrible way to die. The best she could hope for was for the smoke to get her first.

The flames dancing around her house were mesmerizing.

Hypnotizing.

She couldn't take her eyes off them.

They twisted and turned and leaped about, as though merrily enjoying a party. Only the party was her impending death.

"Hey."

A hand clamped on her shoulder, and she let out a startled shriek.

"It's me," a hoarse voice whispered, and she relaxed.

Did it make her a horrible person if she was glad she wasn't alone? She knew that meant that she wasn't the only one who was going to lose their life tonight, but dying alone was everyone's fear, right?

"Let's go." He put his hands on her arm and began to pull her toward the door.

He was right.

They had to go.

And yet for some reason, her feet disagreed.

They wouldn't move.

It was like they'd been glued to the carpet.

"Come on," he urged, tugging harder on her arm.

Her feet still didn't move, but he was bigger than her, and his weight was enough to get her off balance and drag her along behind him as he staggered for the door.

As soon as they stepped out into the hall, her breath was stolen from her, and she broke out into an uncontrollable fit of coughing as her lungs protested the sudden onslaught of smoke. The others were out here too, down on their knees, coughing and wheezing, the sound rising above the crackling flames and adding to her growing fear.

Now that they were in the hall, the reality of how close she was to death became horrifyingly real.

The fire was everywhere.

*Every*where.

It was advancing quickly and was much more prepared for this war than they were. How were they going to get out?

They weren't.

She knew that, but she was still clinging to denial.

Hope was a precious thing, an important thing, a vital thing. Without it, failure was inevitable, but as long as you clung to hope, there was always a chance.

So that was what she did. She grabbed hold of it with both hands and refused to loosen her grip.

The smoke was so thick out here that she could barely see more than a foot or so in front of her. It was like fog, and the only thing that cut through it were the flames.

She felt like she was trapped in hell.

A hand on her head pushed her down low. She'd forgotten that you were supposed to do that if you were trapped in a fire. The smoke rises, so the closer you stayed to the floor, the better your chances were of surviving.

Not that she thought their chances of surviving were very high.

As soon as she got down on all fours, she dragged in several ragged mouthfuls of the marginally clearer air, filling her lungs in preparation of what was coming next.

They all headed for the stairs, which were already partially consumed. The fire was spreading so fast. Like someone had doused the house in an accelerant then struck a match and thrown it in.

That was probably what had happened.

Who had done it, she had no idea, nor did it really matter. She was dead regardless.

Slithering along on her belly like a snake, she thumped painfully down each step. She couldn't see, so she kept bumping her elbows painfully into either the wall or the railings as she tried to avoid the fire as it curled out toward her, trying to snag her in its burning grip. The heat was unbearable, and several times she got precariously close to the flames that were looking for any chance to latch on to her.

Somehow, against all odds, they made it down the stairs.

It was hard to find a safe path through the flames, but she had only one goal: make it to the back door. The door where less than an hour ago she had crept quietly through, hoping that no one heard her.

Now she wanted someone to hear her; she wanted someone to come.

The roaring inferno the house had become would no doubt have woken the neighbors, and she had no doubt that help was coming. Just like she had no doubt it would arrive too late. If she was going to be saved, it would be because she saved herself.

Remaining on her stomach now, she clawed at the floorboards with her fingernails to keep going. Every movement was an effort now.

Her body was sluggish.

Her brain too.

But now that she was so close, she was spurred on.

Her breath wheezed in and out of her chest; her eyes stung, and tears streamed down her cheeks. Her head pounded with a vicious headache, and she was coughing so much that it hampered her ability to move.

But she made it.

She made it to the door.

She wasn't sure how, but she managed to lever herself up onto her knees, and her hands flew like magnets to the handle, and although it was hot and burned her palms, she barely felt it. Gone was fear. Gone for the moment was pain. All she wanted was to get out of this burning, smoke-filled hell and out into the fresh air.

Her hand turned, but nothing happened.

The door didn't open.

She leaned against it, letting her weight push against it, but still, nothing.

Whoever had set the fire had obviously made sure that they wouldn't be escaping.

They were trapped.

They were dead.

"No!" she screamed, banging her fists on the door.

It was so unfair.

She had done the impossible and made it through the fire to the door, and now she couldn't get through it. There was no way she could make it all the way through the house to the front door. Even if she could, she probably wouldn't be able to get through it anyway.

Exhausted, she sank down against the floor.

There was no reprieve from the heat now. It was stifling; the smoke was thick, and there was virtually no oxygen left in the house.

It wouldn't be long.

Her eyelids were too heavy to hold open, and her chest hurt from wheezing so badly.

The flames were licking at her.

Then suddenly, they latched onto her pajama pants.

She gasped in pain as they quickly chewed through the thin material and began to burn through the flesh on her leg.

The pain was unlike anything she'd ever experienced, but it gave her already teetering mind the push it needed to fall into the abyss of unconsciousness.

Her final thought was that it seemed only fitting that she go out in a manner befitting the villains she had always associated so closely with.

She was going down in flames.

* * * * *

6:42 A.M.

"Honey, you're never going to grow bigger if you keep throwing all your food away," Paige Hood told her one-year-old daughter Arianna as she bent to pick up the piece of toast from the floor. Well, calling it a *piece of toast* was a tad bit optimistic. It was really more of a mangled, shredded, soggy, chunk of what had originally been a slice of toasted wholemeal bread with a light scraping of strawberry jelly.

Ari took the toast back and squealed in delight, clapping her chubby hands together and further smashing the once edible food. Before she'd become a mother, Paige never would have thought of picking up a piece of food off the floor and giving it back to her child to eat, but these days she went with the three-second rule or thirty-second rule. So much food wound up on the floor that it seemed like such a waste to throw it all away without at least giving her toddler another go at it.

"Hayley, are you dressed?" she yelled up the stairs to her older daughter, while simultaneously cleaning up the breakfast dishes and packing Hayley's lunch.

It was one of those mornings where they were in a rush. Okay, that was most mornings. With a first grader and a nearly walking toddler, they couldn't be anything but. Thirty minutes ago, her boss had called to tell her that she and her partner had a new case. From what she'd already heard, it was a particularly bad case.

Her husband was a firefighter, and not for the first time their jobs were about to intersect. A family of four had been killed in a fire. It had already been deemed arson, and she and her partner would do everything within their power to find the person who had murdered them.

Since Elias was at work and Ryan would be here to pick her up in about thirty minutes, a friend was coming to pick up the girls and take them to school and day care. With her husband's job as a firefighter, and hers as a detective, their work schedules were usually crazy, so they had come to rely on their circle of family and friends quite a lot. But Paige always made sure that she was available to return the favor—she didn't want to take advantage of anyone.

"Hayley," she called again when she got no response. Her daughter had recently become interested in her clothes. *Very* interested. Paige had thought she'd have at least another five years or more before Hayley hit that stage, but nope, her little girl was growing up quickly and was firmly entrenched in the "obsessing over her outfit" stage.

"Coming, Mommy," Hayley replied, and a moment later she heard the accompanying thundering of footsteps as her daughter ran down the hall from her room to the stairs. Hayley appeared dressed in her favorite pair of jeans that had a star on one knee and a heart on the other, a green sweater, and matching green sneakers. Green was Hayley's favorite color, and half the clothes in her wardrobe were an assortment of every shade of green they could find in the stores.

"Can you do braids, Mom?" Hayley asked, taking a seat at the breakfast bar.

"Braids, honey? Annabelle will be here to pick you up any minute now." Hayley's black hair reached nearly down to her hips. It took a good ten minutes to braid it, and that was ten minutes she didn't have this morning.

"That's okay," Hayley immediately acquiesced, not a trace of disappointment or an impending tantrum in her large blue eyes. Her daughter was one of a kind—the most serious, empathetic, and shy child that she'd ever met. Hayley had had a very rough start in life before they adopted her. They'd done their best with her, quickly gained her trust and her love, and in the year she had lived with them, she had blossomed into a happy and content little girl. While she was still a very emotional child—probably always would be—she never complained or threw tantrums to get her way.

Which was one of the reasons why Paige let her have what she wanted probably more often than she should. It was easy to say no to a sense of entitlement, but to say no to a child who was so sweet and kind and never believed she deserved anything, that was a completely different thing.

"Okay, if we hurry we can get them done, but you eat your toast while I'm doing them," she said as she picked up the comb and some hair ties from the bowl on the kitchen counter—they often did hair down here in the hubbub that was mornings at their house.

"Thank you!" Hayley beamed.

Paige was halfway through the left side braid when the doorbell rang. Balancing hair, the comb in her mouth, and trying to maneuver her six-year-old so that she didn't trip over her, she made her way to the door.

"Morning, Annabelle," she greeted her friend, speaking through the comb.

"Morning," Annabelle returned. "Want me to take over the hair?"

"Do you mind?" She still had to brush her teeth, do her own hair, and grab her boots.

"Of course not; come here, Hayley." Annabelle closed the front door then carefully they did the hair handover.

Leaving Annabelle to take care of the girls, Paige hurried upstairs. She made the bed and pulled on her favorite pair of knee-high boots. The weather had been warm during the day despite the fact it was almost Halloween, but today was supposed to be the first truly cool day of fall. She wrangled her mass of brown curls into a ponytail, brushed her teeth, put on some mascara, lipstick, and a little foundation, then hurried back downstairs to hang with her girls until her partner arrived.

In the kitchen, Annabelle had finished braiding Hayley's hair and finished tidying up. Paige knew that Annabelle was dying to have children of her own. She was a newlywed who had finally married her boyfriend of five years last summer. Annabelle had been a teacher before her life had taken a devastating turn. Now she worked at the women and children's center that they and some friends ran together. Paige knew Annabelle would be a fantastic mother and hoped that she and Xavier got pregnant soon.

"Come here, little angel," she said, lifting Arianna out of the high chair. She probably shouldn't have done it; she was already dressed for work, and Ari lived in a near constant state of mess. Before she even settled the baby on her hip, Arianna had picked up her sippy cup and moved it toward Paige's mouth. She was going through a sharing stage and would often shove any food or drink in her hand into the nearest adult's mouth. Somehow the lid came off, and juice went everywhere, all over her clean work clothes.

She could have lost her temper.

She could have scolded the baby.

She could have cried.

Instead, all she could do was laugh.

After spending years grieving the children a violent assault had robbed her of ever having, and then the disappointment of failed adoption attempt after failed adoption attempt, even now, a year later, most days she still couldn't believe she was a mother to the two most amazing and beautiful little girls on the planet.

"Ari," she groaned, and pressed a kiss to the baby's silky soft head. "Do you have to share your mess around?"

"I'll take the messy munchkin and clean her up." Annabelle laughed and held out her arms to take the happily babbling baby.

Paige handed over her daughter just as a car horn honked outside. "Can you tell Ryan I'll be out in two minutes?" she asked as she ran up the stairs.

Life with children was messy and unpredictable and exhausting, but it was also absolute perfection.

* * * * *

7:33 A.M.

The first thing that struck her as she opened the car door was the smell of smoke.

It seemed to have permeated the entire neighborhood.

Paige scanned the bustling street. The smoldering black structure that only partially resembled a house was at the center. Neighbors lined the streets, held back by police tape, but mostly undeterred by the smell and the grisly scene were standing about in small clumps animatedly discussing the tiny burst of excitement that had rushed into their mundane suburban lives. There were several police cruisers and two fire trucks. The arson investigators would go through the property with a fine-tooth comb, but she and Ryan needed to be here too, especially given what had been discovered inside this completely regular house.

It was upon the fire trucks that her attention settled.

Elias and his team had been one of the trucks called out to the Oliver house.

She knew her husband well enough to know that this particular fire would have been hard for him. Knowing that the family inside had been alive when someone set their house on fire was horrendous, and since they had adopted their daughters, they both found themselves particularly sensitive to any cases involving kids.

When her eyes found Elias, she turned to her partner. "Ryan, I'll be right back."

Ryan followed her gaze and nodded when he saw what she was looking at. "I'll meet you at the door."

Paige gave a quick nod then headed for her husband. "Hey," she said, resting a hand on his arm when she reached him. "You okay?" He smelled strongly of smoke, a smell she was well and truly accustomed to since they'd been married for seven years now. His face was strained, and his chocolate-colored eyes were sober and sad.

"I'm okay, babe," he assured her and touched a light kiss to her lips.

She assessed his face, trying to ascertain if he meant it or if he just didn't want to worry her. She decided it was a little of both.

"Is that strawberry jelly on your neck?" He reached out and touched his finger to a spot on her neck just behind her ear, then brought his finger to his lips and licked it. "It is. You changed perfume?" He snickered.

"Ari." She groaned. More days than not she walked out of the house with a little remnant of the baby's food somewhere on her skin or her clothes, no matter how careful she was. "That baby—"

"Has you wrapped around her chubby little finger." Elias laughed, hooking an arm around her waist and pulling her close to kiss her again, deeper this time.

"I've got to go," she said when he broke contact. "I'll see you tonight."

"Love you."

"Love you too."

As she went to catch up to Ryan, she rubbed at her neck, making sure she got all the sticky jelly off. The smile that always crossed her face when she thought of her girls faded the closer she got to the decimated Oliver house.

A happy family had lived here, and someone had slaughtered them in their sleep.

Being burned to death was a horrible way to die.

She had looked death in the face more times than she wanted to think about. She knew the gut-wrenching, soul-destroying, hope-crushing fear and terror that filled you up inside. She knew the devastation of knowing that you were leaving behind family and friends who would grieve you and wishing you could ease their pain but knowing you couldn't.

"Paige." Ryan lightly touched her arm. "You okay?"

"I want to find who did this and make sure they pay," she said fiercely.

"We will," her partner assured her. Ryan wasn't just her partner—he was her best friend. They had worked with each other for a decade now and been through a lot together.

"Where were they found?" she asked Nam, the arson investigator who was waiting for them at what used to be the front door.

There were four members of the Oliver family. Patriarch Mateo, a forty-two-year-old pharmaceutical rep, matriarch Harper, a forty-one-year-old gym instructor, eighteen-year-old Maya, a high school senior, and thirteen-year-old Penelope, a high school freshman.

"All four of them were in the kitchen by the back door," Nam explained as he led them around the side of the house. The bodies had been removed, but he pointed to a spot in the middle of the blackened debris. "They were huddled together right there. All four of them."

At least the family had died together—they hadn't been alone. That brought her some small measure of comfort.

"The fire was reported quickly. Several neighbors called it in; fire trucks were here within ten minutes, but it was already too late. The fire was too strong and too fierce, whoever set it doused the entire place in an accelerant before they lit it up. The family was already gone by the time the crew got in and pulled the bodies out."

"Smoke inhalation," Ryan murmured.

Nam nodded. "The flames got to them too. Third-degree burns to nearly half of each of their bodies, fourth-degree burns in some places. They likely made it downstairs but couldn't get out the door. They succumbed to smoke inhalation, and once they were unconscious, they were at the flames' mercy."

"They were so close," Paige said. The spot where they had been found was only a couple of yards from the back door.

"Wouldn't have done them any good," Nam reminded her.

He was right.

Whoever had set fire to the house had ensured that even if the family could make it to the door, they couldn't get out. The doors, both front and back, and the French doors leading to the courtyard had all been nailed shut.

This wasn't just arson.

It was murder.

"Were they alive when the fire got them?" Paige asked, shivering at the thought. When she'd been nine, she'd accidentally spilled a pot of boiling water on her foot. She and her siblings had been cooking spaghetti for their parents' anniversary dinner, and her apron had caught on the pot's handle, sending it toppling over and right onto her bare foot. Her parents had spent their anniversary in the emergency room with her. She still vividly remembered that pain. It was indescribable. She had been beaten nearly to death, and the pain from all those injuries combined only just came close to the agony of the burn.

"Probably," Nam said grimly. "Autopsies will confirm or deny it."

The four members of the Oliver family hadn't been the only people inside the house when it was set aflame.

There was a fifth.

An as-yet-unidentified female who appeared to be in her teens.

"Can we go in?" Paige asked Nam.

"I think they've cleared out a safe path through the house, but we need to stick to it. The rest of the place hasn't been checked yet, so beams and floors and walls could still come down."

Carefully, they followed Nam through what had been the Olivers' kitchen into a hall, then turned right and went into what had been the study.

A huge piece of the floor had been destroyed by the fire leaving a large hole.

The hole had been something else before.

A trap door.

The trap door led to a small room.

It looked to be about seven feet deep, and about four feet square.

Unlike the others, the young woman's body hadn't been removed yet. There were metal cuffs around her wrists with metal chains attached. The room appeared to be lined with concrete, and although the study floor had caved in, the rest of the room was intact. There was a metal hook imbedded in the back wall just under the ceiling. The chains that were connected to the girl's manacles hung from it, leaving her dangling feet unable to reach the floor.

The girl's body was naked and blackened with soot from the fire, and although they couldn't get a good look at her, Paige assumed that her body had taken a beating before the fire because littered on the floor of the small dungeon room was a saw, an axe, and a couple of other tools.

This was a torture room.

Hidden underneath the Oliver house.

That one of the family members had put the girl there seemed the only viable possibility.

But which one?

Paige doubted that the youngest daughter would have had the strength to physically get the girl here and strung up. Likewise, the older daughter. The mother was a gym instructor. She was no doubt physically fit and strong, but it wasn't typical female psychology to abduct another female and torture them. That seemed to point to the father as the most likely candidate.

They needed to find out who this young woman was.

They needed to know if there were any other cases matching this MO.

They needed to know if the fire was related to her imprisonment. While it seemed unlikely that someone connected to the girl would burn down the house knowing she was inside, perhaps it was another victim getting revenge or the relative of another victim.

There was one thing that Paige did know. She would do whatever it took to get justice for this girl and for the Oliver family—if they were innocents. If they weren't, then she would make sure that even though they were deceased and couldn't face prosecution, that this girl would not be forgotten. Dead or not, she deserved justice.

* * * * *

8:18 A.M.

Ryan couldn't get the image of the girl in the basement out of his mind.

He couldn't help but see his daughter.

Sophie was only six years old, but she was growing so quickly. The last six years had flown by, and before he knew it, she would be a teenager. His daughter as a first grader was hard enough to handle, but as a teenager, she was going to be a handful. Sophie was a great kid. She was empathetic and caring and curious, but she was also a whirlwind of nonstop energy. She loved to debate and challenge everything they said to her, and she was full of so much confidence that sometimes it almost worked against her. Ryan was grateful every day that his three-year-old son was the complete opposite. Ned was laid back and relaxed. Ryan loved both of his children equally. He just didn't think his nerves could cope with two Sophies.

What kind of kid had the girl in the basement been?

Sweet? Shy? Outgoing? Conceited?

Whatever her personality was, she didn't deserve what had happened to her. No one did.

"Want to start talking to the neighbors?" Paige asked.

"May as well," he agreed. They weren't going to get anything else from the house right now. The arson investigators and the crime scene unit would go through it, and they would find whatever physical evidence was there. The best thing he and his partner could do was try to find a suspect.

The neighbors who'd been milling about in the street when they'd arrived were starting to dissipate as they had to go and get kids ready for school or day care as well as getting themselves ready for work. While Paige had been checking in with Elias, he had surveyed the crowd and taken a few photos in case the killer had stayed behind to survey his handiwork.

"Which house first?" he asked.

"The one across the street."

"Why that one?"

"The Oliver house has a high fence, and the house behind is a ranch. Between the fence and the tall trees, the houses on the left and right don't have a very good view. The house across the street would be our best chance of anyone having seen anything. Plus, I noticed when we got here that there's a stroller on the front porch. They have a little baby, so there's actually a chance that they were up during the night and might have noticed something."

"Nice catch." He grinned at her. Ever since adopting Hayley and Arianna a year ago, Paige had become very aware of anything to do with babies and small children. He couldn't be more pleased for her that things had finally worked out and she and Elias had the family they'd dreamed of. She deserved it. She'd been through hell to get there, but she'd gotten her happily ever after.

They climbed the porch steps, and Ryan rang the doorbell. As they waited, he brushed at his nose. The smell of smoke was strong, and it was slowly infiltrating his nose and up into his head, giving him a headache.

After almost a full three minutes of waiting, the door was finally wrenched open by an exhausted looking blonde with a baby in one arm and a toddler in the other. Ryan remembered when he and Sofia had felt that harried in the early days when they had a newborn and a three-year-old. It wasn't like things got easier the older the kids got, but they did get different. Unless they were sick, Sophie and Ned slept through the night now, and that extra rest certainly helped to face each day. The woman in front of them looked like she hadn't slept in days. Maybe they'd luck out, and she'd been up last night and seen something that could help them.

"Yes?" the woman asked.

"I'm Detective Xander, and this is my partner, Detective Hood." Ryan made the introductions.

"Jen Pickles."

"Can we ask you a few questions?"

"About the fire?" The woman nodded in the direction of the Oliver house and juggled the squirming toddler higher on her hip.

"Yes," he confirmed.

The woman sighed and looked like she wanted to say no because she just had too much on her plate already to deal with anything else, but then she nodded. "Sure." She stepped back and held the door farther open.

"Need some help with those two?" Paige asked.

Immediately, the woman's irritation melted into gratefulness, and she all but shoved the little boy at Paige. "If you could take him, that would be great. I'm trying to feed him breakfast but he's going through this stage where he only wants to eat green things, and the baby has been up all night fussing, and my husband's away on a work trip," she rambled, looking relieved to finally have another adult to talk to.

"Come here, buddy." Paige took the toddler, who immediately began to tug on her hair as they followed the woman through to the kitchen.

"Do you know the Oliver family?" Ryan asked as Paige sat down with the little boy on her lap and began to feed him his cereal.

"Not well. We only moved here just before the baby was born, so about two months ago."

"As far as you know, have they had any problems with anyone in the neighborhood?"

"I don't think so. As far as I know, they get along with everyone. Everyone but themselves."

Ryan arched a brow. "What does that mean?"

"The sisters were fighting all the time. More than once they'd woken one or both of my boys from their naps. The parents too. I think they might have been having some marital problems. A few times when I've taken the boys for after-dinner walks I've heard them bickering."

Interesting.

It seemed there was a lot of animosity between the members of the Oliver family, but had any of that animosity led to their deaths?

"You were up last night?" Ryan asked

"Most of it," Jen replied as she sat beside Paige on the sofa and began to give the baby a bottle. "Between four hourly feeds with the little guy, and then my big guy having trouble staying in his big boy bed, I don't get more than a few hours' sleep any night."

"Do you sit in here with them when they're up?" he asked. This room was at the back of the house, right away from the Oliver house. If she'd been back here she wouldn't have seen anything.

"No, the master bedroom is just at the top of the stairs." She pointed to the staircase in the center of the room, at the top of which he could see a closed door. "If I sit with the boys in here, then it disturbs my husband, so I usually sit in the library."

"Where's the library?" Paige asked.

"At the front of the house," Jen replied.

Perfect.

That was exactly what they wanted to hear.

"Did you see anything last night? Or hear anything? Was there anyone hanging around the Oliver house?" Even after a decade as a cop, he still found his natural inclination was to hold his breath as he waited to see if a potential witness had seen anything useful.

"Tommy was awake and crying. I didn't want him to wake the baby, so even though my husband is away, I was sitting in the rocking chair in the library, desperately praying he would fall asleep so I could sleep a little before the four o'clock feed when headlights flashed through the windows. That wasn't necessarily unusual, but they didn't move right away. The car was there for a good ten minutes or so."

"What time was this?" Paige asked.

She thought for a moment. "Two, I think."

"Did you get up and look out the window?" Ryan asked. If she had gotten a glimpse of the arsonist, then they would have a definitive direction to move in.

Jen nodded. "Tommy wasn't settling in the rocking chair, so I was pacing up and down the room with him in my arms, and when the headlights were still there, I looked out."

"Did you see anyone?"

"Two girls. I think it was Penny."

"Penelope Oliver?" Ryan clarified.

"Yes, she was right in the headlights' beams, and I saw her hair. It's pretty distinctive with all the wild red curls."

"Do you know who the other girl was?" Ryan asked, wondering what the thirteen-year-old was doing out at two in the morning.

"I'm not positive. I think it was her best friend. I've seen the girl around here before, but I don't know her name."

Ryan wasn't sure what that meant yet.

The timing put Penelope and a friend outside the house shortly before the fire. It was called in to 911 a little after two thirty. Assuming Penelope's friend was the same age as her, then neither of them should be driving a car, which meant there was a potential third person there as well.

Although there were three people there, he couldn't see why any of them would start the fire.

Penelope certainly wouldn't have. She was inside the house when it burned down. If she'd wanted to kill herself or her family, for that matter, there were better, less painful ways to do it.

Maybe Penelope and her friend had had a fight, over a boy perhaps, and they had set the fire. It was a possibility, but it didn't feel like a likely one.

Just because two—or three—people had been outside the house around the time of the fire didn't mean that any one of them had anything to do with it.

But at least they had a direction to pursue. They had to track down Penelope's friend and find out what she was doing there and who she was with. Maybe *then* they would get some answers.

* * * * *

1:03 P.M.

"What do you have on the girl?" Paige asked as medical examiner, Billy Newton, entered the room. She loved working with Billy; he was very thorough, and she knew he wouldn't stop until he got some answers that would help them find out who had hurt her. She both admired him as a friend and as a colleague and respected his ability to be so meticulous in his job while raising seven kids, including three sets of twins.

"Have you been able to identify her?" Ryan asked at the same time.

"Not yet." Billy joined them at the table and picked up her uneaten sandwich. Every time she tried to eat something, all she could picture was the final moments of the Oliver family's lives, and that made her sick to her stomach. "She's still a Jane Doe."

"Do you know anything about her?" she pressed. If they were going to identify the girl, then they needed something to go on— however small.

"She's in her mid- to late-teens, probably on the younger side of that. She had brown eyes and brown hair dyed blonde. She had freckles. She had broken her left arm and three toes on her right foot at some point, probably at least five years ago. She was missing two teeth on the top left of her mouth. Again, this wasn't recent as the gums were healed over. The injuries didn't occur at the same time," Billy summarized.

While that was information that may lead them to her identity, given what Billy had just told them, it seemed unlikely anyone would have reported her missing.

"She a victim of abuse?" she asked.

Billy nodded slowly. "There's no way to prove it definitively until you know who she is, but I'd say it's a likely possibility."

If the girl was a victim of abuse, then she could also be a

runaway.

If Mateo Oliver had abducted her, then that would make her a good choice. She might not have been reported missing which meant no one cared about her, and no one was looking for her.

"How badly did he hurt her?" Ryan asked soberly.

Paige wasn't sure she wanted to know that even though she knew it was her job.

"There was only one cut on her," Billy replied.

That was not what she'd been expecting to hear.

"What?" Ryan looked as confused as she felt.

"Only one? There were several tools in there. It looked like he locked her away and strung her up to torture her," Paige said.

"There was only one cut on her arm. It was deep. *Very* deep."

"Deep enough that she would have bled to death?" Paige asked.

"No, but deep enough that she would have been very weak from blood loss. And the cut wasn't inflicted in the last day or so. It was already badly infected. If she hadn't died in the fire, then she would have died within days of septic shock without immediate medical care. Even if she'd gotten to a hospital, she might not have survived. She was already a very sick girl. Also ..." Billy paused like he was about to give them big news—big, *bad* news. "Whoever cut her didn't do it in the basement."

Another thing she hadn't been expecting to hear.

"How do you know?" Ryan asked.

"There was no blood in there."

So, whoever had abducted her might have cut her during the abduction, but then why keep her? Maybe they hadn't realized that they'd hurt her so badly. They had no idea how long she'd been there since they didn't even know who she was. Perhaps she hadn't been there long, and he intended to torture her but hadn't had a chance yet. But if he wasn't going to torture her, then why have the tools there? And why keep her at all? Why not just kill her and dispose of her body?

"Do you know how long he had her based on the progression of the infection?" she asked.

"I would guess that the injury had been inflicted approximately a week ago—no more than ten days."

"Then he had her for a while, but he didn't lay a hand on her." That seemed unlikely. And since their Jane Doe was a young woman, if her abductor hadn't hurt her physically, then she was pretty sure she knew what he *had* done to her. "Was she sexually assaulted?"

"She was," Billy confirmed.

Paige fought against the tightening in her gut. This was a sensitive issue for her. An issue that she, unfortunately, had firsthand knowledge of. But this wasn't about her and what she'd been through. This was about this poor girl who had been abused and then abducted.

She knew Ryan was watching her closely. He'd been there during that dark period in her life when a stalker had been intent on killing her. In fact, he had saved her life on more than one occasion. At first that had made her wary of them continuing to be partners, believing that when he had seen her at her most vulnerable, he wouldn't be able to trust her to have his back, but now she knew that the bond between them had only grown. Her family and his family were the best of friends, and she knew that both would do whatever it took to keep the other safe. What more could you want in a partner?

Pushing aside the feelings that were always just below the surface, kept down by a husband who adored her and two girls who she loved more than life itself, she felt herself begin to calm. Crisis averted. She rarely had panic attacks over what had happened any more, but in the early days, she'd had them regularly.

"Were you able to get any fluids?" she asked Billy.

Beside her, she felt Ryan settle. After working together for so long, they were very attuned to one another's feelings, and when she stressed out, he stressed out and vice versa.

"There were no fluids, but there was extensive damage and tearing; he wasn't gentle with her."

Maybe the tools were just there to torture her when he got bored with raping her and no longer got a rush from it.

"She was right under the house. The study looked like it was Mateo's, so maybe the others didn't go in there much, but the room was sectioned off from the basement. The washer and dryer were down there, so they would have been down there a lot. She must have heard them. Why didn't she call out for help?" Ryan asked.

"Because she couldn't," Billy replied.

They both looked to the medical examiner, waiting for him to elaborate.

"I said he only put one cut on her, but he did do something else to her. I'm no criminal profiler, but I would say he didn't do this to torture her but just as a practical measure to keep her quiet."

"Do what?" Paige asked, sure she wasn't going to like Billy's answer.

"He sewed her mouth and her eyes closed. She *couldn't* call for help," the medical examiner told them.

She'd been right.

She *didn't* like Billy's answer.

The girl was still alive before the fire. That meant she'd been alive when he'd done that to her. Paige prayed she hadn't been awake, fully conscious and aware of what he was doing.

She couldn't comprehend the terror the teenager must have felt when the needle pierced her flesh, stealing from her not only her ability to call out for help, but also to see where she was and what he was doing.

"Do you have anything else for us, Billy?" Ryan asked grimly, just as affected as she was by what the girl had gone through.

"I might once I get a chance to do the full autopsy, but

nothing else right now. Good luck," Billy said, and took the last of the sandwich with him as he headed out of the room.

"We might have two separate cases here," she said once she and Ryan were alone. "Mateo is the most likely candidate as our Jane Doe's assailant, but he didn't set the fire. There was no way he could have nailed the doors shut, poured the accelerant around the house, lit the match, then gotten back inside. Without DNA, there might never be a way to prove conclusively that he was her abductor, but he was certainly the only one in that house who could have raped her. The fire might have nothing to do with that."

"We should run what we know about the Jane Doe and see if any other cases have a similar MO. If we do find other cases, it could be a victim who escaped or who he attacked earlier on before he progressed to killing."

She'd thought the same thing. They'd do that, but for now, they had to focus on the family and which member had been the target. There was a chance that this was random, and if it was, then the arsonist would kill more families. But for now, they had to work under the assumption that someone wanted to murder the Oliver family.

"We need to look at each member of the family. We already know that Penelope was out and up to something last night. According to the school, her closest friend is a Dakota Canton, so it's likely that she was the friend Penelope was with." They were going to interview the fourteen-year-old later today. Maybe she could tell them what was so important—or secret—that Penelope had to take care of it in the middle of the night. "Penelope was the daughter who didn't fit in. She was younger than her classmates, very intelligent, but not popular. Older daughter Maya was the opposite. She was very popular at school but not as smart. Both Mateo and Harper seem to have been well liked at their workplaces, and no one in the family has any criminal record."

"Do we know anything about the girls' biological parents?"

Ryan asked.

Both Oliver girls had been adopted when they were very young. "Both adoptions were closed. Maya was only a newborn when she was put up for adoption. Penelope was slighter older, almost a year when the Olivers brought her home." Her daughters had been five and a few months old when she and Elias adopted them, but the similarities between her family and the Olivers were disconcerting. "It seems unlikely that thirteen or eighteen years later one of them would come back and kill their biological child and her adoptive family."

The family wasn't getting along, and at least one of them was harboring a secret worth killing over.

But which one?

* * * * *

3:26 P.M.

So far, what they'd found on the Oliver family didn't get them a single step closer to finding their killer. If nothing else, the family was pretty good at putting up a good front. No one thought they were perfect, but no one really had anything bad to say about them.

What Jen Pickles had told them appeared to be true. Apparently, Maya and Penelope hated each other. They fought at home, they fought at school, they fought over everything. It seemed that Penelope was jealous of Maya's popularity and Maya did whatever she could to rub her sister's face in it. Sibling rivalry was common, and Paige didn't think that it held the power to lead to something of this magnitude.

"Good afternoon, Mrs. Canton," she said as the woman opened her front door. "I'm Detective Hood, and this is my partner, Detective Xander."

"Good afternoon," the older woman returned, clearly

displeased by their presence.

On the phone, she had all but told them that her daughter was a little angel and that she wasn't going to be able to help them. She had adamantly denied that her child would have been out at two in the morning, and school and music were all Dakota cared about. Whatever Penelope and Dakota had been up to, their parents were clearly in the dark.

"Dakota has her violin lesson at four," Mrs. Canton informed them as though a music lesson trumped a murder investigation.

"Mrs. Canton, your daughter's best friend and her family were murdered. We have an eyewitness who placed your daughter at the scene just thirty minutes before the fire was started. Surely, you can understand why it's imperative that we speak with her." Paige kept her tone calm even though she was annoyed by the woman's attitude.

Looking only mildly rebuked, Mrs. Canton led them through into a formal lounge room. The woman was in her mid-forties, with slightly graying brown hair pulled back into a neat bun, pearls at her slender neck, and a beautifully coordinated and expensive looking skirt and blouse outfit. She looked as though she believed this entire thing was beneath her and not worth her time. Paige hoped the daughter, at least, had some common human decency to want to help find who had just horribly murdered four people.

"I'll get Dakota." She left them in the lounge room while she collected her daughter. Obviously, she didn't just yell out through the house like Paige always did when she wanted Hayley for something.

"Hard to imagine a daughter of a woman like that setting fire to a house full of people," Ryan said quietly.

"She seems pretty cold though, very indifferent to her daughter's best friend's murder."

"Yeah, but lighting that fire, she'd probably have messed up her manicure."

Paige snickered at her partner's joke. It wasn't that either of them didn't care about what had happened to the Olivers—innocents or not, they didn't deserve to die like that. And Paige's best friend had been murdered, so she certainly empathized with the friends and family left behind, but sometimes the only way to break the tension and make sure the cases they dealt with didn't consume and destroy them was to make the occasional joke.

"Detectives, here's my daughter." Mrs. Canton stood in the doorway with a tall, slim girl who looked much younger than her fourteen years. Dakota had yet to mature. Her chest was flat, her long hair hung in two braids, her skin was smooth and without the usual teenage blemishes, and the pair of glasses perched on her nose looked like something a nine-year-old might choose and not a girl of fourteen.

"Would you like your mother to remain with us while we ask you some questions, Dakota?" she asked. Since the girl was a minor, she had the right to have a parent present while they spoke with her. Since she was not a suspect at this time, they weren't required to have her mother remain. Considering the girl was a teenager and teenagers were notorious for keeping things from their parents, they might do better if the mother left them alone.

"Yes," the girl replied immediately.

However, Mrs. Canton shook her head. "You'll be fine, and I have things to attend to." The way she said it made it clear that she felt them being here was an imposition on her apparently busy life.

"But, *Moooom*," the girl whined.

"No buts and I don't like that tone, Dakota. I'll be in the study, should you need me," Mrs. Canton informed them and then left.

Dakota remained where she was in the doorway. She looked sullen and uncooperative, and Paige wondered if it was just because she was grieving or because she had something to hide—or a combination of the two. The girl could refuse to speak with them if she chose, and it looked like she was close to doing that.

"Dakota, how long had you and Penny been friends?" she

30

asked, hoping if they started the conversation out in a nonthreatening manner, it would help to put the girl at ease.

"Since the first day of junior high," Dakota replied, taking a tentative step into the lounge room. "Is she really dead?"

Denial was common when a loved one was taken away suddenly without warning. "She is."

"In—in a fire?" Dakota took another step forward.

"Yes. Someone set her house on fire. You girls were close?" she asked gently.

Dakota nodded and came and joined them, taking the sofa opposite where Paige and Ryan were sitting. "Best friends," she murmured. "Neither of us fit in. I'm too tall and the other girls made fun of me, called me names. And Penny skipped a grade; she was smart, but the other girls would tease her about being a robot because she wasn't so good at making friends. They'd tease her about her hair too. They'd call her Crazy Carrot Top."

Being misfits had obviously brought the girls together and caused them to bond, but two teenage girls who felt left out—and one of them being highly intelligent—they had been up to something. Something that may have gotten Penelope killed. And if Penelope and her family had been killed because of whatever the girls had done, then that meant Dakota and her family were also at risk.

"Where were you last night, Dakota?" Ryan asked.

"At home in bed," the girl answered quickly. *Too* quickly.

"Before bed what did you do?" Paige asked.

"Homework then I went straight to bed. I was tired, and I wanted to get a good night's sleep because we had a big test today," Dakota replied as though she had memorized her lines.

"We have a witness who saw you at Penny's house," Ryan informed her.

Every ounce of color drained from the teenager's face.

"Just half an hour before the fire was started," Ryan continued.

"What were you two doing, Dakota?" Paige asked.

"I—we—uh—" the girl stammered, then blurted out, "it was Penny's idea."

"What was Penny's idea?" Paige asked.

"She was tired of being unpopular. We just started high school, and she didn't want to waste it being left out of everything. She just wanted to find a way to make the other kids like us."

"What did you two do?" Ryan asked.

"Penny hacked into some of the teachers' computers and got the answers to tests, then we sold them," Dakota explained in a small voice, her gaze fixed firmly on her neatly folded hands resting in her lap.

That sounded like something a smart but unpopular teen might try to do to make people like them, but it didn't sound like something that would get her killed in such a violent manner. Paige sensed there was more to this story.

"Did one of the kids get caught and get angry with you?" she asked.

"No."

"Your mother didn't mention anything. Does she know?"

"No."

If no one had been caught for the test stealing and selling scam, then maybe it had nothing to do with the fire.

But if it had nothing to do with the fire, then why were the two girls outside the Oliver house at two in the morning?

"Someone knows though, don't they?"

Dakota gave an almost imperceptible nod.

"Who?"

Scared brown eyes looked up at them. "One of the teachers whose computer we hacked found out."

Paige was feeling more confused with every question she asked. "Well, if a teacher knew, then why didn't they report you to the principal?"

"Because he was scared."

"Of you two?" Ryan asked. "What did you girls do to him,

Dakota?"

"It was Penny's idea," she said defensively.

"What did you do to him?" Ryan repeated.

"We went to his house straight after school one day. Broke in. Put rose petals all over his bed and lit a million candles. Then I hid in the closet with my phone, and Penny waited on his bed in some sexy lingerie she found in her mother's dresser. Then when he came in, she pounced on him and kissed him. I videoed the whole thing."

"You made it look like he was involved with Penny sexually," Paige said, shaking her head in disbelief. If that video got out, not only would the teacher lose his job, but he would also likely face prison time and spend the rest of his life on the sexual offender's registry.

"Yes." Dakota dropped her gaze again; her pale cheeks had morphed from white to burning red.

"You blackmailed him into keeping quiet."

"Yes."

That was certainly something that might make someone angry enough to kill. These girls staged a scenario to make an innocent man look guilty—and ruin his life in the process. "When did this happen?"

"Two nights ago. We went back to his house last night because Penny was afraid that we didn't have enough evidence. She thought that if he showed the evidence he had on us and then told people we were just trying to blackmail him then people might believe him. So she hacked his computer again and sent herself messages asking her to come over to his house after midnight. We even got a copy of his key made, so it looked like he'd given it to her." Dakota began to cry as she realized that their childish games might have cost her friend her life. "I'm sorry. We shouldn't have done it. Everything just spiraled out of control so quickly. Penny was so determined that he wasn't going to ruin her plan. All she cared about was being popular, and I—I—I just went along with it because I was tired of always getting left out and being bullied."

If their scheme had gotten her friend killed, then that was something Dakota was going to have to live with for the rest of her life. Every choice you made had consequences. The plan might have been Penelope's, but Dakota had gone along with it. She had been prepared to ruin a man's life just to be included and invited to the best parties.

"What was the teacher's name?" Ryan asked.

"Mr. Brownlee. Ian Brownlee."

Ian Brownlee had just become their number one suspect.

Just like Dakota was responsible for the choices she had made, so was Ian Brownlee. If he had set fire to the Oliver house, killing not just Penelope but her entire family, then he would be held accountable.

* * * * *

5:41 P.M.

They said revenge was a dish best served cold, but he had to disagree. Revenge was a dish best served hot. *Burning* hot.

He couldn't be more pleased with how last night had gone.

It was his first time starting a fire. He'd had no idea he would actually like it. He'd just done it because it seemed like the most practical option. In the beginning, he'd even been a little apprehensive about it. What if he messed it up? What if he accidentally set himself on fire? What if the fire just fizzled out and didn't really burn anything? It turned out he shouldn't have worried. Starting the fire had been exhilarating. Who knew fire could be so much fun?

He wasn't what any psychologist would call a classic serial killer. There were no dead animals or bed-wetting or fire starting in his past. He was just a guy who had been pushed too far and been left with no option but to strike back.

What choice was he left with?

None.

It was how life worked, right?

If someone did you wrong, then you paid them back. Karma. That was what people were always talking about. Doing a bad deed meant you were owed one in return. That was all he'd been doing when he'd nailed the doors shut, doused the house with gasoline, and struck the match, dishing the Olivers up a big serve of karma.

They deserved it.

Despite what anyone else might think, the Olivers weren't good people. If he hadn't done it, then sooner or later someone else would have.

Almost twenty-four hours had passed, and he hadn't regretted anything so far. He was still riding a high, remembering the crackling of the fire as it consumed the house, the feel of the heat on his face, and the mesmerizing way the flames danced about as though they were co-conspirators and were pleased to be able to get him his revenge.

The only thing he regretted was that he hadn't been able to hear them scream.

He'd thought he'd be able to. He knew they were alive in there when he set the house on fire, and he'd thought he'd be able to satiate his anger with the screams of the person who had hurt him. But he hadn't been able to hear anything but the fire. It had been a little disappointing, but nothing too major; in the end, his goal had been met. They were dead now.

He hadn't wanted to leave.

It hadn't taken long for neighbors to be awoken by the fire and to call for help, and he'd still been hiding in the bushes watching in a near trance.

Even once fire trucks descended on the house he hadn't gone far. He'd just blended in with the neighbors who had all come out of their houses to observe what was going on.

In the end, he had only left because he had to.

If it were up to him, he'd still be there staring at the blackened shell of what had once been the Olivers' house. He liked knowing that he had done that. That he had taken control of his own life, of his destiny. He wasn't going to let anyone play games with his life.

Not. Going. To. Happen.

He wasn't a bad guy. He wasn't a sociopath or a psychopath. He was just a regular guy, living a normal life. Whatever he did, he did it to his best ability. He had family and friends; he was fit and healthy and took care of his body. He took care of his mind as well and was successful at pretty much everything he tried. He wasn't a monster. He'd never seen himself as someone who would set fire to a house full of people. And he still didn't. What he had done was for the sole purpose of getting revenge on someone who had wronged him, and he had enjoyed it—he couldn't deny that.

It was satisfying to know that he'd gotten the upper hand and turned the tables on someone.

It was satisfying to know he wasn't a pushover, that he'd fought for himself, for what was right.

He wasn't sorry for what he'd done, and if he had to do it again, then he would in a heartbeat.

* * * * *

7:26 P.M.

"It's almost bedtime, sweetheart," Paige told Hayley as she stuck some pins through the bear ear to attach it to the headpiece of the costume.

Hayley said nothing, which was a sure sign that she wanted to negotiate but didn't want to be rude or disobedient. Because of how she had spent the first five years of her life, she was a child who was always very conscious of her actions and the impact they would have on herself and other people.

"Hayley," she prompted as she threaded her needle. She had never sewed before she had kids, but she had quickly found that she really enjoyed it and had made several dresses for the girls and was even having a go at making their Halloween costumes. Hayley was going to be a bear, and Ari was going to be a honey pot. It had taken almost two months for Hayley to decide what she wanted to be. They had gone through the Disney princesses and superheroes and all the popular shows for kids her age, but she hadn't been interested in any of those. She wasn't like other children. She had lived through something horrific, and the impact on her would be long-lasting, possibly irreversible.

"Mommy, are you doing Arianna's costume next?" the little girl asked, taking the scissors Paige passed her and put them back in the sewing box.

"Yes," she replied, even though she knew Hayley already knew that; they'd discussed it after dinner when Hayley had said she wanted to help finish off her bear costume.

"Can I help?" Hayley asked tentatively. "I want to help you make Ari's costume really beautiful." Her blue eyes glowed excitedly—she didn't often get excited. It wasn't that she was an unhappy child; she was affectionate and sweet and did well in school and loved to dance, but she was very serious.

Paige smiled at her daughter. It was a school night, and she really should send her off to bed so she'd be well rested, but she enjoyed spending time with her. They'd already grown close, and Paige cherished these moments because when Hayley was a teenager, they might not have as many. "You can stay for thirty extra minutes," she told her, "but you only get one bedtime story tonight. Deal?"

"Deal." Hayley beamed and held out her hand to shake on it. "Mommy, can we use sparkly gold sequins to write 'honey pot' on

Ari's costume?"

"Sure, do you want to go and grab them from the spare room?"

"Okay." Hayley bounded up and went darting out of the room, almost crashing into her father as Elias finished putting the baby to bed and came to join them.

She watched her daughter skip off, so happy to do something for her little sister that Arianna wouldn't even realize or remember. Her girls were already so close, but she couldn't help but think about the Oliver family. They, too, had been unable to have biological children of their own and had ended up adopting two beautiful girls. Two girls who had ended up hating each other.

Did the fact that they were adopted play into the animosity?

It was something she worried about constantly.

Not so much with Hayley. She would always have some memories of the hell she had escaped, but Arianna would never remember her biological father. What if that ended up becoming a problem? What if she wanted to learn where she had come from—about her bloodline? Paige knew she wouldn't lie to her daughter. When Ari was older and wanted to know the truth, then Paige would tell her.

Then what would happen?

The worry that someone would want to reclaim her daughters was still there. Not as bad as it had been at first. She would never forget the first time she had taken the girls to see their sisters, although they weren't biologically related they had lived together as a family for five years and Paige knew they still thought of themselves as sisters. She had been petrified that Eliza would want them back, that Hayley would want to stay with them and not come back home.

If that had happened, it would have killed her.

Thankfully, it hadn't.

The kids had had a blast, having ice cream and playing in the snow, but when she'd gotten tired, Hayley had come over and settled on Paige's lap just like she always did. And Eliza had pulled her aside before leaving to thank her for giving the girls the life they deserved.

Bit by bit the fear of them being taken from her was fading, but now, the fear of them leaving on their own was growing.

Arianna could be angry about how she was conceived; she could take that anger out on the rest of them, driving a wedge between her and them.

"What are you thinking?" Elias's voice jerked her out of her thoughts as he perched on the arm of her chair and wrapped his arm around her shoulders.

"The Oliver girls were adopted," she said softly. It wasn't like it was any secret to Hayley that they had adopted her, but she still didn't like to talk about it much when Hayley was about.

"So?"

"They hated each other."

"So?"

"What if ..." Paige trailed off, knowing she sounded stupid but unable to use that knowledge to squash her fears.

"What if that happens with our girls?" Elias asked.

She nodded.

"Honey, we're not them. So, we both have adopted daughters ... so what? That doesn't mean our family is going to turn out like theirs did. We love each other, we love our girls, and they love us. Relax. Don't go looking for trouble where there isn't any." He pressed a kiss to her temple.

He was right.

She knew that.

And yet ...

"Found them, Mom," Hayley announced, returning with a bag full of sequins that she used to make dance costumes and occasionally when they did crafts.

"Great, let's pop your costume down and put these on Ari's." She gave her daughter a big smile, but the little girl wasn't fooled.

She was almost too intuitive for her own good.

"Is everything okay?" Hayley asked joining her at the table.

"Fine," she promised. It wasn't really a lie; everything *was* fine. It was just her insecurities acting up. "Do you want to try sewing some on?"

Hayley's eyes searched hers, seeking reassurance that she apparently found because she relaxed and nodded. "Is it hard?"

"Not for a smart girl like you. Come sit here." She patted the seat in front of her and Hayley came to perch in front of her. Paige put her arms on either side of her daughter and took her hands. "Okay, we take the threaded needle, and we put the sequin where we want it." They took one of the shiny gold sequins and put it over the words she'd already sewed on a few days ago. "Now, we take our needle, and we put it underneath the material, and we push it up and through the middle of the sequin." Paige guided Hayley's small hand and helped her push the needle through.

"What next?"

"Next we're going to go around the sequin and then push the needle back through the material. Then last, we go back up again on the other side then back down through the middle of the sequin."

"Can we do another?" Hayley asked as soon as the first was secured.

"Of course."

For the next thirty minutes, they sewed on enough sequins to fill the letter H. By the end, Hayley was pretty much doing it on her own.

"Okay, sweetie, time for bed," Paige announced when the H was done.

"Can I help you do the rest tomorrow?"

"Yep. I'll finish off your costume tonight, then tomorrow after I get home from work, you and I will finish up Ari's."

"Go brush your teeth and get your jammies on, and Mommy

and I will be up in a few minutes to tuck you in and read you a story," Elias told her, and Hayley went running off upstairs.

When she'd first moved here, Hayley had been afraid of going upstairs by herself. Paige had expected the child to have nightmares, but she hadn't. Well, she'd had the occasional one, but she had settled in so quickly. Ryan's daughter, Sophie, had been a big part of that. Sophie was so confident and seemed to have known without being told that Hayley needed some help in learning how to be a kid and had taken her under her wing.

Her daughter had come so far in the last year. And getting to be her mother had helped her to heal as well. Hayley and Arianna had been two bright, shining lights at the end of a very dark time in her life. They had helped her own nightmares to fade away because she had a purpose in her life now. She had people who relied on her. Knowing that had made sure she got herself the help she had needed to recover from the devastation her stalker had caused.

Elias was right.

Their family was nothing like the Olivers.

Her family was strong and full of love.

Her family was the best thing that had ever happened to her, and she couldn't imagine her life without them.

OCTOBER 29TH

8:09 A.M.

Paige hadn't expected to be coming here first thing this morning.

The plan when she and Ryan had gone home for the night had been to interview Ian Brownlee and then go from there. So far, he had a motive to kill Penelope Oliver, but they didn't know enough about him yet to say for sure that he was capable of wiping out an entire family in such a horrific manner.

One thing in the teacher's favor was he hadn't run.

He had turned up to work as usual today, so he either had nothing to hide or he was smug enough to believe that he'd never be caught. Maybe he thought that Dakota would never talk because she'd be implicating herself in a crime. The girls had hacked a computer and stolen information that wasn't theirs. Then they'd committed blackmail. It didn't matter if it had been Penelope's idea, Dakota had gone along with it. She was just as culpable. If found guilty, they would be facing potential prison time. Ian could have been banking on Dakota keeping quiet.

Whatever his reasons, he was at work, and they had an appointment to speak with him at lunchtime.

The change in plans had come about because Billy Newton had called around six this morning, waking Paige from a deep sleep, to tell her that he had managed to ID the girl in the basement. Her name was Danielle Terry—she was fifteen years old, and just as they had thought, she was a victim of abuse.

Danielle had been removed from her home for the first time at the age of six. She'd been bounced back and forth between living with either of her biological parents and foster care. About a year ago she had been removed from her home permanently after her father had killed her mother, then attempted to kill her too.

"Sorry to come by so early," Paige said when the door was opened by an older woman with gray hair pulled into a ponytail and a warm, easygoing smile.

"No problem at all, come on in," she greeted them, waving them in and leading them down to a kitchen where a fire was raging in a fireplace. "I know it's not that cold, but I just love fires," Sally Shield told them, bustling about and collecting mugs and spoons, producing a teapot and a coffeepot, as well as a plate of toast. "Eat up," she urged, setting down an assortment of jars of jelly.

Even though she'd already had breakfast with the girls before leaving home, Paige felt the woman would find it impolite if they didn't have something, so she poured a cup of tea and took a piece of toast, spreading a little blackberry jelly on it.

"Thank you, Mrs. Shield," she said as she took a bite of toast.

"No need for formalities, dear, call me Sally. Come on, dear, take some toast," she urged Ryan, who complied and spread a generous amount of apricot jelly on his toast.

Sally Shield had been Danielle Terry's foster mother and the one who had reported her missing. In less than five minutes, the older woman had put her at ease. She was warm and caring, and Paige was wondering why Danielle had run away from this place. Although she was eternally glad she had adopted Hayley and Arianna before they had entered the foster care system, if they had, this was exactly the kind of home she would have wanted them to land in.

"You reported Danielle Terry missing," Ryan said.

Sally's shiny brown eyes clouded over. "Yes. She had only been with me for a couple of weeks before she ran. It wasn't unusual for teens who'd been through something traumatic like that."

"Was she happy here?" Paige wanted to get a feel for the girl so they could figure out how she had been taken.

"Yes and no. I raised five kids of my own. I spent thirty years as an elementary school teacher, and when I retired a few years ago, I knew this was how I wanted to spend the rest of my life, giving a home to children who had never had one. Over the last three years, I've probably had around three dozen kids come through here; a few have stayed for months, before either being adopted or aging out of the system. Some have only been here a few weeks or even a few days. I can give these children a safe, warm, comfortable home, but I can't make them accept it."

"Is that what happened with Danielle?" Paige asked.

"She knew she was safe here, but she couldn't believe it. She kept waiting for something bad to happen to her just like it had every other time. She'd get taken away from her parents, placed in a foster home, begin to do well, then her mother would leave her father to get her back, and she'd go back there, only for her mom to take the husband back every time. She had no sense of stability, and she didn't see being here to be any different than any other place she'd lived. I tried with her. I spent as much time with her as I could. I encouraged her to focus on her school work, and I encouraged her to have friends. I also encouraged her to try extracurricular activities to find something she could be invested in, but I couldn't get her to break out of her self-imposed shell."

"When did she run away?" Paige asked. They wanted to try to get a timeline in place.

"Today's the …" Sally trailed off, looking to them for the date.

"The twenty-ninth," Ryan supplied.

"Then she ran on the twentieth. That's right … it was the day of my oldest son's birthday. We had a big party. All the family and all the foster kids were there. We even had a few of the children who used to live here come. Danielle was invited, but she wouldn't come. I didn't force the issue; I knew she needed time. I just wished she had given herself the time." Sally looked both sad and disappointed like she felt that she had personally failed the girl.

"When did you notice she was gone?" Paige asked.

"When we got home. I put the younger kids to bed and then went to check on her. When I opened the door to her room, her bed was neatly made, and all her clothes were missing from the closet. I called the police immediately and reported her missing, but part of me hoped she'd come back on her own."

"Is there anyone who Danielle was close to who she might have confided in? Another kid here, a friend from school, a teacher she trusted?" Paige asked, particularly interested in the teacher side of things. No, it didn't look like Ian Brownlee would have had access to the Oliver house to put Danielle there, but the teacher was connected with a member of the Oliver house; therefore, she wasn't discounting anything at this point.

Sally pondered this for a moment, her head cocked thoughtfully, then she nodded. "There was another girl. A friend from school, I think. I'd seen her around a few times. She must have lived near here because some days they would walk home together, but they never came in. One day I went out and introduced myself, told Danielle she was welcome to have friends over, this was her home, but they both declined."

"Do you know the girl's name?" Ryan asked.

"I believe it was Amy. I'm sorry, I don't know her last name."

They would contact Danielle's school as soon as they finished up here and see if there were any Amys in her classes. Mateo Oliver might be dead, but if he had abducted, raped, and tortured Danielle Terry, the girl deserved to have her assailant formally identified.

"Were there any teachers at her school who took an interest in her?" Paige asked, still pushing the Ian Brownlee issue. For all they knew, the thing with Penelope was just a coincidence, and he and Mateo had been in on abducting Danielle together, and that was why he'd burned down the house.

Sally thought again, then said, "There was an English teacher.

He contacted me recently. Actually, it was *after* Danielle ran away. He was questioning me about whether she had cheated on a test."

Cheated on a test?

Paige exchanged glances with her partner whose interest looked as piqued as hers.

"Was the teacher's name Ian Brownlee?" she asked.

"Yes," Sally said slowly. "I think it was."

That was the confirmation they needed to discuss Danielle Terry with Ian later today as well as Penelope and Dakota.

"As far as you know, did Danielle know anyone with the last name Oliver?" Ryan asked.

"I don't think so," Sally said. "Oh, no, wait." Her eyes glowed as she obviously recalled something. "There was a girl with that last name. She was tutoring Danielle in math. Danielle was struggling with that class, and I spoke to the school and asked if there was someone they could recommend to help her, preferably another kid from the school. I thought it might help Danielle to fit in. The girl was a redhead, and I can't remember her first name. I think she only came a couple of times, but her last name was Oliver."

That had to be Penelope Oliver. "How did she get here? Did she walk? Take the bus? A parent drop her off and pick her up?" Paige asked, hoping it was the latter.

"I believe one of her parents came and picked her up. What happened to Danielle?" Sally finally asked, her face clearly saying she didn't really want to know the answer.

As much as Paige didn't want to tell the woman what had happened to the girl she had clearly cared deeply about, she knew the woman deserved the truth—with as little detail included as possible. No one needed to know that a child who had been in their care had been brutally raped and tortured.

* * * * *

10:14 A.M.

He was panicking.

They were on to him.

He wasn't cut out for this.

Ian wished he knew how much the cops knew.

They had to know something because he had received a phone call from a Detective Hood telling them that she and her partner needed to speak with him and made an appointment for lunchtime today.

Lunchtime was quickly approaching.

The morning had passed in a blur. He couldn't remember anything that had happened in his classes. No doubt the kids had noticed—probably taken advantage of his distraction—but he didn't care.

He might be going to prison.

What happened in his classes was of little consequence in the grand scheme of things.

He nervously paced up and down the teachers' lounge. What were the cops going to ask him? What was he going to tell them? What had they heard? What did they know?

Did they *know*?

It was possible they did.

They might know everything.

Were they really coming to arrest him?

He shouldn't have done it. Ian was man enough to admit that. It was a mistake—a terrible, horrible, regrettable mistake. If he could take it back, he would, but he couldn't, and now it looked like he was going to have to live with the consequences.

But living with the consequences meant most likely spending the rest of his life in prison.

Prison.

Him in prison.

In prison.

The thought was terrifying.

He wouldn't.

He couldn't.

He'd rather die than go to prison.

Not that death was a much better option.

There seemed to be only one thing he could do.

He had to leave.

Now.

He spun on his heel and crashed straight into someone.

For a moment, he panicked. It was the cops. They were already here. They would slap handcuffs on him and shove him into a police car and drive him off to prison, and he would never again walk the earth as a free man.

Ian was debating whether to attempt making a run for it when he realized it wasn't one of the cops he had walked into; it was one of his colleagues.

"Ian? Everything okay?"

"Yes." He faked a smile at Enid, the ninth-grade math teacher. "Well, no. Not exactly. I'm … I'm not really feeling very well."

Apparently, he also looked like he wasn't feeling very well because Enid's eyes crinkled in concern. He shouldn't be surprised, the way his stomach was twisting and turning itself into knots. He felt awful right about now. He'd thought he could do it. At first, it had been so easy. He'd felt so good; revenge had been sweet, but now he didn't care about revenge. What good was it if he couldn't enjoy it because he was locked up?

"I was thinking I might just get someone to cover the rest of my classes today and go home, try to sleep off whatever I'm coming down with," he told Enid.

The older woman clucked sympathetically. "Drink some warm tea with lemon and honey, and get plenty of rest," Enid said as she hurried off to enjoy her break before she had to return to a room full of crazy teenagers.

"Will do," he said, quickly gathering his things. He had to get out of here while he still had a chance. He'd go home, pack his bags, drain his bank accounts and then flee. He had no idea how to go about starting over, but figuring it out was better than staying here and waiting for the inevitable to happen.

He didn't have a choice.

It was now or never.

The cops would be here in a couple of hours, so he had to go now. If he hurried, he could be on the road before they even knew he'd gone.

* * * * *

12:23 P.M.

"No Amys in the entire sophomore class," Paige told her partner as they headed toward Ian Brownlee's house. When they had arrived at the school to speak with the teacher that Penelope Oliver and Dakota Canton had been blackmailing, they'd been told that he'd gone home sick.

Sick, or he was running.

She hadn't made up her mind yet whether the teacher was just panicking because he knew that if they found out about the blackmail they'd be suspicious of him, or if he was panicking because he was guilty.

"Any in the freshman, junior, or senior classes?" Ryan asked.

"There are two Amys at the school. Both are seniors, but neither fit the description Sally Shield gave us—one is Asian, and the other is Latina. Maybe she knew Amy from a previous foster family she stayed with; she could go to another school."

"We can look into it after we talk to Ian," she said. As much as she hated to admit it because she believed that Danielle Terry deserved justice, that case had to take the back burner to the arson. They had to assume that Mateo was responsible for Danielle's abduction, but he was dead, and the person who had set the Oliver house on fire was still at large and potentially still a threat to others. Finding him had to take priority over proving Mateo was Danielle's kidnapper.

"If he ran, then it definitely points to him being the guy we're looking for," Ryan said.

"But then why not run right away? Why pretend he's cooperating and then back out at the last minute? He knew we were going to be there at one, and yet he didn't ditch work. He went, did the first two classes, then bailed."

"Maybe he wanted to catch us off guard. He appears to be trying to work with us, that lowers him down a few notches on our radar, then he takes off. He thought he had a little extra time, we got to the school early with the intention of getting him on edge and unprepared, he probably thought he had enough time to pack and run before we even realized he was gone. That could have been his plan all along. He might have had his things packed and already be on the run," Ryan said.

That was true.

But Paige was hoping that they'd find Ian Brownlee at his house. If he ran, it did make him look guilty, but she wanted hard proof. If this was payback for the blackmail, then Dakota and her family were still at risk.

"Is Hayley excited about her first Halloween?" Ryan asked, abruptly changing the topic.

"She is, not so much for the candy, but just to do things together as a family."

She and Elias had adopted the girls just a couple of days after Halloween last year, so Hayley had never experienced it before. Over the last year, they'd had a lot of firsts. The girls' first Thanksgiving had been a quiet one. Hayley had still been anxious around large groups of people, so instead of spending it with their families, she, Elias, Hayley, and Arianna had celebrated it together. By Christmas Hayley's confidence had been growing, and she'd been excited to put up a Christmas tree for the first time. While she hadn't requested anything, the ritual of putting out milk and cookies for Santa and carrots for the reindeer, then seeing in the morning what had been left for her had been very intriguing to her. They'd spent Christmas day with all their extended family, and Hayley had thoroughly enjoyed her first large family gathering. By the time Easter rolled around, she had enthusiastically attended an Easter egg hunt party at Ryan's house.

Paige really couldn't be more thankful for everything that Ryan and Sofia's daughter Sophie had done for Hayley. Without Sophie for a friend, Paige was sure that Hayley wouldn't have adjusted nearly as well as she had.

"She's also very excited about the party. She's been helping me make her costume, and she can't wait for everyone to see it." After they took the girls trick-or-treating, they were going to a party at the Xander house. Paige had been concerned that it might be a little too scary for her very sensitive and emotional daughter, but Hayley had been very enthusiastic about it, and she was so proud to see how her daughter was growing.

"Sophie wants to decorate the house already." Ryan laughed. "She's been hounding Sofia every day since October started to do it. She's pretty much worn her down, and they've been putting up a few things every day after school. Our house and yard are going to look every bit as scary as a real haunted house. I just hope the weather holds."

She did too. She wanted to continue to encourage Hayley to try new things and keep coming out of her shell. "I think it's the next left," she told Ryan, transitioning her mind from family back to work. When she'd first returned to work after adopting the girls, it had been hard. She'd been away from work for almost three months, both recovering from the injuries her stalker had inflicted as well as helping the girls settle in, and that break had made it hard to step back into the darkness that was her job after spending so much time basking in the light that was her new family.

"There it is," Ryan said as he pulled the car to the curb in front of a small Cape Cod house.

"Car in the drive," she noted. "Maybe he really was just feeling sick and went home early."

"Maybe."

They climbed out of the car and Paige surveyed the house as they walked toward the front door. The yard was fully enclosed, and she wondered if Ian owned a dog. If he did, they'd have to be careful. A dog wouldn't understand that its owner was a suspect in a murder investigation. All it would know was that Ian was its master, and it would protect him if it thought he was in trouble.

The gate was unlocked, and when they opened it she got a clearer view of the house. The curtains were all drawn so she couldn't see anything inside, but the outside of the house was a mess. The yard wasn't tended to, the house was in bad need of paint, and one of the trees in the front yard looked dead and like it could be ready to fall over with one strong gust of wind taking an entire side of the house down with it.

Ryan knocked on the door, and they waited in silence to see if Ian would answer.

He didn't.

"Think he could be sleeping?" she asked.

"That or he's gone." Her partner put his hand on the door handle, and the door swung open. "Mr. Brownlee?" Ryan called out.

There was no answer.

"We should go in and check that he's all right," Ryan said with a small smile. It was a good way to get around probable cause. As far as they knew, Ian Brownlee *was* sick and might have collapsed. They'd just go in and check the house to find him, and whatever they saw as they were searching for him, they saw.

"Split up? You take upstairs, I'll take down?" Paige asked. It could be riskier to not stick together, but it depended on how dangerous Ian was and how he was likely to react if he wasn't just lying somewhere ill. And how dangerous Ian was depended on a lot of things. Had he only been out for revenge when he'd started the fire? Was he innocent and just scared they'd found the blackmail video? Was he violent and the fire wasn't the first crime he'd committed? In the end, it didn't really matter. Even the most docile of animals would claw and bite and thrash and fight for its life when backed into a corner. She'd been hurt on the job before, but it never made her afraid. She'd known the risks when she chose this job, and although she was always as careful as she could be, she knew that there was always the chance that the next case could be her last. Despite that, she couldn't imagine doing anything else.

"Sure thing," Ryan agreed, heading for the stairs.

The inside of the house was as messy and uncared for as the outside. Ian had never been married and had no children. It appeared living alone allowed him to be the slob he wanted to be.

She was just walking through the kitchen when she heard a noise outside.

The dog she thought he might have or Ian?

"Ryan, outside," she yelled out as she pulled out her gun and headed for the back door.

It wasn't locked, so she slid it open and stepped out into an overgrown yard.

It appeared empty but there were several outbuildings that Ian could be hiding in should he still be here. There didn't appear to be a dog as none came running over, and there was no doghouse or dog bowls or toys.

Paige carefully made her way toward the closest building, a shed that appeared to be three quarters falling down.

Just as she stepped up ready to open the door, something slammed into the back of her head.

She saw stars.

Everything grew fuzzy.

Her stomach felt like it was tumbling in a myriad of

somersaults and taking the rest of her body along with it.

She staggered, her hand seeking something solid to steady her and she fell against the side of the shed, sending the dilapidated building crashing down.

Her gun flew from her hand as she fell, and although her vision was blackening, and she was clinging to consciousness with everything she had, she crawled about searching for it.

"Ian," Ryan yelled out as a door slammed.

Paige couldn't find her weapon, but her partner should have his.

A shot rang out right above her head.

Ian Brownlee had found her gun.

* * * * *

12:52 P.M.

Ryan couldn't see his partner.

As soon as Paige had yelled out that she heard something in the yard, he had come running downstairs, but he hadn't made it before he heard a gigantic crash.

He'd picked up his pace, and by the time he'd burst through the back door, one of the sheds was lying in a heap on the ground, and a man whom he presumed was Ian Brownlee was searching for something on the ground.

Paige's gun.

Ian must have found it because all of a sudden, a shot boomed through the air and pain shafted through his shoulder.

Ignoring the pain, Ryan was forced to dart backward behind the door.

Doing it was one of the hardest things he'd ever been forced to do because his partner was still out there, and since Ian had gotten her gun, she was obviously hurt.

The pain in his arm was growing, and his life metaphorically flashed before his eyes. Happy days as a kid with his parents and brothers, meeting and falling in love with Sofia, adopting Sophie, Ned's birth, all milestones, and he wanted to be there to celebrate the rest of the milestones that were yet to come.

One wrong move and both he and Paige would wind up dead.

Knowing what he had to do, Ryan carefully eased the door open. Ian was throwing aside pieces of debris, looking for Paige.

"Put the gun down, Ian," he called out. For the moment, he had the advantage. Ian still held the gun, but his back was to Ryan. If Ian wanted to fire, he'd have to turn around, which would give Ryan enough time to fire first.

"I'm not going to prison," Ian yelled back.

"If you've done nothing wrong, then you won't," Ryan said, although it was now clearly a foregone conclusion. Ian had fired at and shot a police officer, and possibly killed Paige, even aside from whether he had anything to do with the fire at the Oliver house.

"It's already too late." Ian sounded hopeless, and that wasn't a good thing. If he felt like he had nothing to lose, he could do something reckless.

"Don't do anything you're going to regret, Ian." Ryan was trying to keep his gaze focused on Ian while also scanning the debris for signs of Paige. Where was she? Was she already dead? She had to be hurt to have lost her weapon, but how badly?

"I already did," Ian said softly.

Then without another word, he spun around, gun in hand, but before either he or Ryan had a chance to fire their weapons, Paige darted up from the rubble and slammed something into Ian's back.

The man cried out and dropped the weapon, which Paige just managed to kick out of the way before she teetered and then fell to her knees.

With the weapon out of Ian's reach, Ryan pulled out handcuffs and secured the man who was crying quietly, because of what he'd done and not because of pain, Ryan suspected.

As soon as he knew that they were safe, he went to his partner. "Paige?"

"I'm okay. He got me in the head." Her voice was weak, but she'd been able to take Ian down, so he hoped that meant she didn't have a concussion.

He knelt beside her and tilted her head to the side so he could see. The back of her head was coated in blood, which continued to flow from the wound. He needed to get something to stop the bleeding.

"Ryan, your shoulder." Paige lifted a shaking hand to point at his arm.

"It's fine," he told her. Adrenalin was still buzzing in his system, and he wasn't feeling any pain yet. That would come, but right now, what he was more worried about was having to tell his wife what had happened. Sofia wasn't a drama queen, and she knew his job was dangerous and didn't try to pressure him to find a safer job, but that didn't mean that she didn't worry about him.

"He shot you." Paige looked from his arm to where her gun lay discarded.

"Skimmed my shoulder," he corrected, sure it was true. If the bullet had plowed through him, he'd be in a lot more pain. As it was, it was just a dull throb. "I'll go find towels for your head to stop the bleeding. You call in what happened."

Paige looked like she was going to object but apparently was feeling sufficiently woozy to stay put. Ian hadn't moved and was still crying quietly, so Ryan gave his partner his weapon and ran inside, finding a couple of towels and then returning.

"Here, hold this to your head." He lifted Paige's hand and pressed it to the towel he'd put against her wound. "How are you feeling?" he asked as he wrapped the second towel around his shoulder.

"A little dizzy," she admitted. "You?"

"A little sore." It looked like the wound on his shoulder was already starting to clot. Head wounds bleed a lot more, so it was Paige rather than himself that he was more concerned about at the moment.

It only took a few minutes for sirens to fill the air. Ryan was checking Paige's head again as EMTs and officers came through the house and out into the backyard. His partner's hands were still shaking, so he took over keeping pressure on the wound.

"Read him his Miranda rights," he told the officers, then waved the medics over. "She was hit in the back of the head; it's still bleeding pretty badly."

His phone began to ring, so leaving his partner with the paramedics, he moved a few feet away and answered.

"It's Stephanie," a voice said through the phone.

Stephanie Cantini was a friend and a crime scene tech, one of the techs who'd been recovering evidence from the Oliver house. If she was calling, that had to mean she had good news for him, and he could definitely use some good news right now. "What's up, Steph?"

"I have something for you." He could hear the smile in her voice.

That was exactly what he wanted to hear. "What?"

"I found some DNA in Harper Oliver's car."

"Like blood or hair?"

"Like seminal fluids."

Seminal fluids? He had to assume it wasn't Mateo's because Stephanie wouldn't waste either of their time by calling him to tell him that Harper had been having sex with her husband. That raised the possibility of an affair. Mateo and Maya both had their own cars, and Penelope was only thirteen, so she was too young to drive. That meant that it was most likely Harper who'd been having sex in there. "You get a match?"

"I did."

"Who?"

"Ian Brownlee."

That was the last thing he had expected to hear. "Ian Brownlee? Our suspect? The man who Harper's daughter was blackmailing?"

"The very one. His DNA was in the system because he donated a sample to eliminate himself as a suspect when an ex-student was raped and murdered."

That raised even more possibilities.

Had he really been having sex with Penelope in the car? Was the blackmail story that Dakota had told them true or was it just that—a story? Or was Ian having an affair with Harper?

So many questions and the answer to them was just being hauled off to a police car. Ian would be taken, booked and processed, then once they were finished up here, he and Paige would go and talk to him. If they were lucky, he'd be in the mood to open up; after all, he had nothing to lose.

"Anything else, Steph?"

"Nothing right now, but I'm still going through things. I'll let you know the second I get anything else that can help you."

"Thanks, Steph." Ryan disconnected and returned to where EMTs were wrapping a bandage around Paige's head. "She all right?"

"Yes," Paige replied immediately.

It wasn't that he didn't believe his partner, but he wanted a professional's opinion on that.

"No concussion. We put in a couple of stitches. She'll be fine," one of the medics summarized.

Paige shot him a look that clearly said *I told you so*, then asked, "Who was that?"

"Stephanie found evidence that Ian Brownlee was having sex with someone in Harper Oliver's car," he informed his partner.

Her brown eyes widened, and her mouth dropped open, then she winced as the medic tightened the bandage. "Does she know who with?" Paige asked. "I mean, I guess it was probably Harper, but it could have been Maya or Penelope."

"No, but we have Ian. He was going to try to run. He hit you over the head and shot at me. He was going to kill us both and flee; if that isn't an indication of guilt, then I don't know what is."

"Let's go talk to him now." Paige tried to stand, but a medic pressed a hand to her shoulder and held her in place.

"Just sit for a bit and take it easy. You may not have a concussion, but you still took a hard blow to the head. You're going to be a little faint and woozy for a bit," the EMT warned.

"Before we do anything else, we need to call Sofia and Elias to let them know what happened before they hear from anyone else." Paige's husband was a firefighter, his brother was a cop, and their friends were all cops, so word could easily get to one or both of their spouses before they had a chance to break the news.

"Yeah, you're right," Paige agreed, looking as distinctly reluctant to make the call as he felt.

Ryan dialed his wife's number while the paramedics came to check out his shoulder and prayed that she took the news well.

* * * * *

2:40 P.M.

Amy was scared.

Not the kind of scared where you found a spider in your bedroom or you were going on a ride at an amusement park or you were worried you were going to get a speeding ticket. This was the kind of scared that held you in an icy grip, invading every part of your body and your mind. It made your stomach churn constantly so that even if you were hungry, you probably wouldn't be able to keep food down. Where you felt both exhausted and wired at the same time. Where you were constantly on edge waiting for the worst to happen, and then when it did, waiting for something even worse to come next.

She couldn't go on like this.

She'd rather be dead.

Amy hurt so badly.

Every single inch of her body. Her hands had been chained above her head for so long they'd gone numb, and she wouldn't be surprised if the limbs died from lack of oxygen. Her head ached from where he'd hit her, and there was a long gash on her thigh that still oozed blood if she moved about too much.

Not that she was doing much moving anymore.

Her body was too weak. Now she spent her days alternating between hanging by her arms from the chains that secured her to the ceiling, allowing them to take her weight and bearing the pain through her shoulders because she was too exhausted to do anything about it, and balancing on her tiptoes until her legs cramped and she couldn't do it any longer.

This was not how she had expected things to turn out.

Things had finally been getting better. She'd thought that everything was finally going to work out and she was finally going to have everything she'd ever wanted.

And then it had all gone wrong.

So, so wrong.

With nothing else to do, she had tried to figure out just when things had turned, but so far, she hadn't been able to come up with an answer. If she could go back and do it over, she would likely wind up right back here. She never learned from her mistakes. Never.

Part of her wished he would come back just so she wouldn't be alone.

Her whole life she had wished she was alone. That people would just leave her be and let her live in peace and quiet. Only it turned out that when you had nothing but peace and quiet, it nearly drove you insane. Now she'd give almost anything to have some company, even if the only company she could have was his.

Her stomach growled, adding some noise to the small room she was trapped in.

Well, she couldn't see to know that the room was small, but she felt it. Before he had brought her here, he had wrapped a strip of cloth so tightly around her head it cut painfully into her eyes. It stole her vision, and she had found that her other senses had grown stronger. She could hear things she'd never heard before, and she could smell every little thing. It didn't make up for losing her sight though. She wanted to be able to see where she was, to see *him* when he finally returned.

Her stomach growled again. Her hunger came and went in waves, but worse than the hunger was the thirst. Her mouth was dry. The rolled up T-shirt he'd stuffed in there made it worse. It was too large for her mouth and prevented her from closing it, so saliva dribbled out and down her chin, draining any moisture left in her mouth. Every molecule of her body screamed out for water. The thought was never far from her mind. She even dreamed about it whenever she dosed off.

Maybe that was the plan. Maybe it was how he was going to kill her. Just leave her here to die of dehydration. She couldn't be all that far away. She hadn't felt the need to pee in a long time. She had a headache and was dizzy. She could feel her heart thumping too quickly in her chest, and she was breathing rapidly. Amy knew that her symptoms were likely a combination of dehydration and blood loss from the deep wound on her leg.

The T-shirt he'd used to gag her was her own, which left her half naked. So far, he'd left her bra on as well as her pants and shoes, but she didn't know if he'd used her T-shirt only because it was convenient or because it was a precursor of what was to come.

She prayed it was the former.

But since she didn't know, it only fueled her fear.

At first, her fear had been everything.

It had consumed her.

Now it had dulled.

Everything had dulled.

Lethargy had taken the edge off everything.

She was just hanging around, waiting to die.

Amy wondered absently where Danielle was and whether she was still alive. Was she strung up in chains in some small, dark room? Had he done something worse to her? Was he going to come and do worse to her? Or had he gone for good? Had he been arrested? Had he been killed? Was he going to just watch her die? How much longer could she last? If he didn't mean to just let her die of dehydration, how was he planning on killing her? Was he going to torture her first? Rape her, maybe?

So many questions.

Just thinking of them all made her head hurt.

She didn't want to worry. She didn't want to think. She didn't want to wonder. She didn't want to do anything but rest.

Her legs gave way, and she let out a muffled cry as her body jerked forward and fresh pain stabbed her numb arms and shoulders.

This was hell.

Tears squeezed out from behind her blindfold and rolled slowly down her cheeks.

She'd spent her whole life being helpless and not in control, and she hated that she was once again strung up and at someone else's mercy. Or lack thereof. Amy was ready to just get it over with and die already.

* * * * *

4:39 P.M.

Paige swallowed a couple of pain pills and massaged her temples. She'd had a headache ever since Ian Brownlee had hit her over the head. It was only by some miracle she'd managed to remain conscious, and as soon as Ryan had distracted him by coming out of the house, she'd grabbed a piece of rubble and darted around the side of the closest building.

In the end, it had come down to split-second timing.

If Ian had turned just a little quicker and got off a shot, Ryan could be dead. Or if Ryan had been forced to kill Ian to protect himself and her, then their answers would have died along with him.

Thankfully, everything had worked out as it had.

All three of them had walked away with only minor injuries, and now they were about to go and interview Ian.

"Want some?" she asked her partner, holding out the bottle of painkillers.

"I'm good," Ryan replied. "Your head okay?"

"Yeah, I still feel a little fuzzy, but I'm all right," she assured him.

"You sure?" Ryan checked.

Paige rolled her eyes at him. Sometimes he forgot she was his partner and not just his friend and tried to play the overprotective card. She knew that it was because he had seen her close to death before, thanks to her relentless stalker, but just because she understood didn't mean it wasn't annoying. "You got shot," she reminded him.

"A bullet skimmed me," he corrected.

She shrugged as she stood. "Toe-may-toe, toe-mah-toe."

He rolled his eyes right back at her, and she laughed. Getting to spend every day at work with her best friend—her husband excluded, of course—made her job even better.

"Come on, Ian Brownlee is waiting for us," she said.

Gathering their papers, they headed to the interview room where their number one suspect was waiting. Ian had declined to have a lawyer present, so they didn't have to worry about one jumping in and shutting them down.

"Mr. Brownlee," Paige said as she and her partner entered the room. She felt extremely satisfied to see the man wince as he turned in his seat to look at them. The blow to the head he'd given her had left her with four stitches and a headache that would no doubt last for days, so it seemed only fair that she'd hit him in the back with a piece of wood and given him some bad bruises.

Ian's blue eyes watched them closely as they took their seats at the table across from him. So far, he had only been charged with the assaults on herself and Ryan. They wanted more information before they officially charged him with the Oliver house fire and murders.

"We know you've been having sex in Harper Oliver's car," Ryan announced.

Ian's face drained of all color.

"I guess we can add statutory rape to your quickly growing list of offenses," Paige said, watching him closely for his reaction. They still didn't know if he'd been having sex with Penelope or her mother.

His pale face flushed bright red. "I never had sex with Penny," he said vehemently.

"Not what we heard. Or saw," Ryan goaded. Dakota had shown them her copy of the video she had filmed of Penelope throwing herself at Ian, and it was extremely convincing. If she hadn't known better, Paige would have thought that the teacher had seduced his student and they were having a sexual relationship.

If it were possible, Ian turned an even brighter shade of red. "They were blackmailing me. Penny and her friend, Dakota Canton. They faked the whole thing. Broke into my home and set everything up, then accosted me as I came through the door." Ian spoke so fast, his words blurred together, but what he'd said fit exactly with what Dakota had already told them. At least they knew he wasn't lying about that.

"Why didn't you come back at them with proof of the cheating?" Ryan asked. Paige wanted to know the answer to that as well. Yes, the girls had a video of him kissing Penelope, but that could easily be brought into question when he countered with evidence the girls had been hacking computers and selling stolen tests answers.

"What cheating?" Ian's brow crinkled in confusion.

That wasn't the response she was expecting. She exchanged glances with Ryan. Had Dakota been lying to them? Had the girls really been selling stolen tests or were they up to something else? Or was Ian lying to them now, trying to play some angle they hadn't figured out yet?

"Then why were they blackmailing you?" Ryan asked.

Ian squirmed uncomfortably like he knew he had to give them the answers they were after, but he wanted to delay the inevitable for as long as possible. "I wasn't having sex with Penny. That whole thing was the girls setting me up. I was sleeping with Harper." He dropped his gaze and refused to look at them.

Again, that fit with Dakota's story that there was nothing real between Penelope and Ian, Penelope just wanted to use the video against him. But why? That was the question they needed to answer. "Why was Penelope blackmailing you then if you didn't know that they were hacking into teachers' computers and stealing tests?"

"She wanted me to stay away from her mother."

That seemed like a lot of trouble to go to just to try to break up your mother's affair. Was there more to it than that or was that all Penelope had truly wanted? From what they'd heard, the sisters weren't close with each other, but maybe Penelope had been close with her mother and didn't want to see Ian hurt her, or with her father and didn't want to see her mother hurt him. "Was Penelope close with her mother? Or her father? Did she want you out of the picture so they wouldn't break up?" Paige asked.

"Penny hated her mother," Ian explained. "She didn't want me to stop seeing her mother so her parents could live happily ever after. She wanted me to stop seeing her mother because she knew that I made Harper happy, and she didn't want to see that."

From the sounds of things, the entire Oliver family had been in shambles. "So, she knew that you and Harper were having sex?"

"In love," Ian corrected. "And I wasn't the one who approached Harper. She came to me."

"Why would she do that?" Ryan asked.

"Because of Mateo."

Maybe Mateo had been abusing his wife and daughters before he moved on to Danielle Terry. "Was Mateo abusing her?" she asked gently.

"What? No. Harper never mentioned him hurting her or the girls, and I never saw anything to contradict that. It wasn't Mateo beating Harper that drove her away. It was the fact that he had a son."

A son?

They hadn't heard anything about a son from anyone else they had interviewed. Which didn't mean a son didn't exist.

"Mateo had him as a teenager. He didn't have anything to do with him, and he signed away his paternal rights. He didn't want to be a father. Until later. When he and Harper first got married, they wanted kids right away. They kept trying and trying, but Harper couldn't get pregnant. She didn't know that Mateo had a son before they met, and when she found out, it created a wedge between them. They started growing further and further apart, and at a parent teacher conference at the end of the last school year we got to talking, and it just grew from there. This wasn't just an affair." Ian eyed them defiantly. "We were in love. She was going to divorce Mateo. She'd already told him, and they were sleeping in separate bedrooms."

That Ian had set the fire was seeming less and less likely. He already had the woman he wanted. It didn't seem likely he'd kill her and her family. Unless Penelope had already shown the video she'd made to her mother and Harper had broken up with him. Maybe he'd lashed out and set the fire in anger to punish both

Penelope for engineering the demise of his relationship and Harper for ending things.

Her partner was apparently on the same page, because he said, "You loved Harper. Penelope made the video to blackmail you into breaking up with her mother. You end things or she shows her mom, and Harper ends things. Is that what happened?"

"No," Ian replied firmly.

"Then why did you run?" Paige asked.

"When we were at your house earlier, you said you weren't going to prison, and that it was already too late, you'd already done something you regretted," Ryan said. "Did you start the fire? In anger maybe, and then regretted it?"

"I didn't start the fire. I would never hurt Harper, even if she had broken up with me, which she hadn't. I told you, I love her. Loved," he corrected, and from the sadness that filled his eyes, Paige believed it. "I wanted something on Penny. If I'd known about this test stealing thing I would have used it, but I didn't, so I used Harper's phone to get into her bank accounts and drained Penny's college fund. I planned to put the money back as soon as Penny deleted the video," he said earnestly. "But then they were killed, and I thought you'd find out that I'd taken the money and you'd be suspicious. I thought that was why you were coming to talk to me, so I was going to take the money and flee, use it to start over. It's what Harper would have wanted."

She was fairly certain Ian was telling the truth, and he wasn't the killer. "Do you have an alibi?"

"No. I live alone. Penny and Dakota came over around midnight. They tried to break in. Somehow they'd gotten a key, but I had the chain on the door, so they couldn't get inside. I was going to bring Penny into my office at school the next morning and tell her about the money, get her to back off. I watched the girls out of one of the upstairs windows, and once they left, I went to bed. I didn't hear about the fire until the next day. I don't know how to convince you that I didn't do it," he said, looking at them forlornly.

"Do you know who Mateo's son is?" Paige asked. If the son had a grudge against his absentee father and the family he'd created all the while excluding him, then that could be a motive to burn them all alive.

"I know his name, but that's it. If you want to know more about him, then I suggest you talk to Maya's ex-boyfriend. Harper wasn't the only one who knew about Mateo's son. The whole family knew. Maya was dating him."

* * * * *

6:02 P.M.

"Are you all right?" Elias closed the front door behind him and practically ran down the garden path to his wife.

She looked okay.

Well, besides the white bandage wrapped around her head.

Ever since she'd called him to inform him that she'd been injured on the job, he'd been anxious and distracted. He'd almost lost her so many times before, and just hearing that she was all right wasn't the same thing as seeing for himself that she was whole and mostly in one piece.

For as long as he lived, he would never forget walking into the intensive care unit to see his wife lying in a bed, completely still, on a ventilator, hooked up to a dozen machines, her face covered in bruises with one eye swollen closed, and with a bandage much like the one she wore now wrapped around her head.

That day was the single worst day of his life.

Before then, he'd never really thought that they were mortal.

Of course, he'd known they were going to die one day, but it wasn't until that moment when he'd seen the woman he loved so vulnerable and close to death that it really sank in. They both had dangerous jobs; he was a firefighter, and she was a cop. Either one of them could go to work one day and never come home.

From that day on, he had never taken life for granted again.

"Elias?" Paige touched her hand to his cheek, her brown eyes worried.

She was worried about *him*.

When she'd just been hit over the head and nearly killed by some suspect who'd rather kill cops and flee than face the consequences of his actions.

But she hadn't been killed.

She hadn't.

She was standing right here in front of him, a little blood on her burgundy coat, her brown curls in a wild halo around her head, and her nose crinkled in that cute thing she did when she was worried about him or their girls.

He loved her so much.

So much that sometimes he physically ached when something happened to hurt her.

"Come here." He reached out for her and drew her against his chest, laying his cheek against the top of her head, carefully avoiding her wound. He'd come so close to losing her. His grip tightened, holding her so close, he was sure he must be hurting her, but she didn't protest, just wrapped her arms around his waist, rested her forehead against his chest and snuggled closer.

For him, this was heaven.

Holding the woman he loved in his arms, feeling her heart beat against him, her breath warm against his neck. This he could do forever.

"I love you." He kept one arm wrapped around her, holding her close, their bodies melded together, he hooked a finger under her chin and tilted her face up so he could kiss her. She tasted like the mango lip balm that was her favorite, as well as the licorice that she was obsessed with eating. It was an odd combination, but he loved it because it was Paige.

"I love you, too," she said when he tore his mouth away from hers only because she'd been hurt, and she really should be inside resting, not standing outside in the cold in the middle of their front yard.

He wanted to get her inside, and yet, at the same time, he was worried about how Hayley would handle seeing her mother hurt. His oldest daughter was a very sensitive child, and she took things very seriously. She was a worrier. Elias was concerned that she was going to freak out when she saw the bandage on Paige's head.

"You're worried about Hayley," Paige said, reading in his face what was going on inside his head. It was one of the things he loved most about her.

"I am."

"Does she know?"

"Yes. You know what she's like; she knew something was wrong as soon as I picked her up from school." He hadn't planned on telling his daughter until Paige was home so Hayley could see for herself that her mother was all right, but his little girl was too perceptive for her own good.

"We have to start trusting her," Paige said. "She's a smart girl, and she's grown so much in the past twelve months. We can't always be giving her the impression that we're worried that she can't handle things. That little girl has handled more in her six years than most people do in an entire lifetime. We want her to know how strong she is. I don't ever want her to doubt herself and the amazing person that she is."

Paige was right.

Their daughter was strong, and he wanted her to know it. He wanted her to grow up to be an independent woman who knew her worth and never let another person convince her that she wasn't worthy.

"You are an amazing mother. Our girls are so lucky to have you." He brushed his lips across his wife's.

"I'm the lucky one," she said. "So lucky to have a husband who loves me and supports me, and who loves our children so completely."

From the look on her face, he wondered if she was still worrying about the Oliver family. Elias didn't care that there were a few similarities between their family and the family that had been killed in the fire. He loved his wife and children. They were his world, his reason for getting up each day, and there wasn't anything he wouldn't do for them. He picked Paige up and began to carry her toward the house.

"Elias," Paige groaned, but couldn't quite hide her giggle and wrapped her arms around his neck, resting her head against his shoulder, and he knew how badly scared she'd been. She was the bravest person he knew. What she'd been through because of a stalker's incorrect assumptions was horrendous, and yet she had never given up. She fought every day to overcome what had happened to her. She'd fought to let go of her fears. She'd fought to let go of her insecurities. She'd fought to find happiness and peace, and he would never let anyone take that from her.

"Mommy." Hayley ambushed them the moment they stepped through the door. Annabelle, who had come over to babysit if he'd had to leave for his shift before Paige got home from work, was right behind her with the baby in her arms.

"I'm okay, sweetheart." Paige pushed gently at his shoulders, so he set her on her feet, but kept an arm around her waist and held her against his body. "It's just a bump on the head, kind of like you got when you fell off your bike last summer when you slipped in that puddle. You remember?"

Hayley nodded but looked like she was debating bursting into tears, which she had done a lot of when she first came to live with them, or deal with it like the incredible, strong girl she was.

For almost a minute the jury was out, and they all waited to see the outcome.

Then Paige gave her an encouraging smile, and Hayley visibly relaxed. "I'm glad you're okay, Mommy," she said and came to wrap her arms around Paige's waist.

Paige leaned down and kissed the top of her head. "Did you guys have dinner already?"

"Annabelle made spaghetti and meatballs," Hayley replied.

"Thanks, Annabelle," Paige said. "You've got to go and get ready for work, honey," she told him. "Hayley, why don't you go and get your jammies on and we'll watch a movie and eat some popcorn." Paige went and took Ari from Annabelle's arms.

"Okay," Hayley said excitedly and dashed off upstairs.

"I'm glad you're okay, Paige." Annabelle gave her a hug, then collected her things and headed off.

"Wish I could hang with my girls tonight." He loved his job, but nothing beat an evening snuggled on the couch with his family.

Paige grinned at him, balancing the baby on her hip. "How about after the Halloween party you and I do a little snuggling of our own."

With kids in the house now they got a lot less adult snuggling time than they used to. "I'm going to hold you to that," he told her, kissing the sensitive spot just under her collarbone that he knew was going to make her shiver. And like clockwork, she did.

She lightheartedly glowered at him. "You'll pay for that one."

"I look forward to it."

"I'm ready, Mommy," Hayley announced, sprinting down the stairs.

"Kiss Daddy goodnight, sweetie," Paige told her, and Hayley threw herself at him and kissed his cheek when he lifted her up.

Elias kissed his baby, who patted his cheeks with her chubby little hands, and then his wife. This was what life was all about. Family. No matter what life threw at them, his family just kept getting stronger. Paige didn't need to worry. The Olivers were nothing like their own little family. Their family was as close to perfection as it was possible to get.

OCTOBER 30TH

1:16 A.M.

He parked his car in the next block and slipped out. Dressed all in black, he became one with the night.

He had always liked the night.

To him, night was freedom. The dark was made for hiding, and although he had never felt that he was a bad person—recent events excluded—he had always appreciated that about the dark. While other children had feared the inky darkness, sleeping with nightlights on and wanting to sleep in their parents' bedrooms, he was asking for blackout curtains so he could make his room dark even during the day. For him, the dark was peace, and right now, it was also his protection.

In the event that anyone happened to be up and watching him, he strode purposefully toward the house he had parked his car in front of. Part of succeeding in life was faking it. If you looked like you belonged and weren't doing anything untoward, then people believed that you belonged and weren't doing anything untoward. Appearances mattered. Confidence mattered. If you didn't feel it, then you had to fake it. Should anyone see him, they would just assume he was returning home late from work or the airport or the gym or the store or someplace completely innocent.

As soon as he was close to the house, he darted around the side, through the gate and into the relative safety of the backyard. There was still a chance that someone could be up in the house and would notice him but the chances of that happening weren't particularly high. Most people were in bed at one in the morning, and even if they weren't, they'd have to be at a window looking out. Then they'd have to notice him which wasn't too likely with him wearing all black and hiding in the dark.

His biggest problems weren't someone seeing him. There were motion sensor lights and dogs, and both would draw attention to him. A dog had almost been his downfall the other night. He'd been just a couple of houses away from the Oliver house, sneaking through backyards, when one had noticed him and immediately came trotting over to see who he was and why he had suddenly turned up in its territory. By some miracle, the dog hadn't barked. If it had, the whole plan would have been ruined. It would have roused its owner, they would have come. He could have been discovered or, at the very least, enough of a ruckus would have been caused that it wouldn't have been safe to proceed.

Good luck had found him that night, and he prayed it would follow him again tonight.

Scaling the wooden fence in the backyard of the house he'd pretended he belonged in, he stayed up on top as he made his way along it and toward the house he had business with tonight. His balance was pretty good, and he felt like it was safer to stay up higher, away from any pets. He didn't want a dog barking at him, and he certainly didn't want one biting him.

He didn't have far to go. Six houses along and on the opposite side of the block from where he'd parked his car. He needed to be close to it to be able to make a quick getaway, should it no longer be safe for him to remain and watch his handiwork, but not so close his vehicle would be associated with the arson.

The night was cool with a pleasant, refreshing breeze. With winter quickly approaching and the cold weather finally creeping in, several people had started lighting their wood burners and open fireplaces. The scent of burned wood lingered in the air, a delightful precursor to tonight's events.

It didn't take him long before he was jumping off the fence and down into the yard of the house he was after.

The Canton house.

Home to Sylvia and Earl Canton and their fourteen-year-old daughter Dakota.

Tonight's fire would be different than the last one.

While that one had been part self-preservation, it had also been part revenge. This one was pure self-preservation. He had nothing against Dakota Canton and her family, but the girl had talked. She must have seen something that night when she and Penelope had been standing outside the house talking. The cops had to have spoken with her, and whatever she had told them had turned them in his direction.

He couldn't allow that.

There was no way he was going down just for fighting back and standing up for himself.

Quietly, he did a circle of the house, checking every window to make sure there were no lights glowing inside. He didn't want to be caught when he was this close. Everything looked as it should be. He couldn't see or hear anything, but the longer he was here, the riskier things got. He had to move quickly.

Kneeling down, he slid his backpack off and unzipped it, pulling out his tools. The first thing he had to do was make sure that even if the family were able to make it to the doors, they wouldn't be able to get through them. With nails and a hammer in hand, he headed to the back door. Last time he'd been terrified that someone would wake at the sound of the hammering and come to see what was going on, but no one had.

It was Lady Luck.

She was on his side because what he was doing was right.

Protecting yourself was what life was all about.

Survival of the fittest.

He believed that God created the world but for those who believed in evolution, that was the entire basis of that belief system, wasn't it? The weak perished and the strong survived. Well, *he* was the strong one, and he was going to stay that way.

It didn't take long to hammer some nails into both the front, back, and side doors. Because he wanted to make sure that everything went off without a hitch, he also put a few nails in all the first-floor windows.

When he was satisfied that the house was secured, he returned to his backpack and pulled out the can of gasoline. Circling the house slowly, he poured a generous amount all around the bottom of the house, splashing some up the walls for good measure. Then because he wanted to make sure that the fire spread inside the house as well as surrounding it, he threw the gasoline can through a window and into the house. He wore gloves, so he wasn't worried about the crime scene people finding his fingerprints. He wasn't entirely sure whether fingerprints survived fire, but he'd decided he would rather be safe than sorry.

Since he'd just shattered one of the windows, there was a chance that one of the Cantons had awoken at the sound, so he had to keep moving.

Pulling matches from his pocket, he struck one against the side of the box and tossed it at the house.

Immediately, a fire roared to life.

The flames took hold quickly, and in less than a minute they had spread and created a dancing ring of yellows and oranges and reds encircling the building.

It was so beautiful.

He'd never thought about fire being beautiful before. He'd never really thought about it at all, but after setting two fires now, he was definitely starting to feel like he was slowly moving from arsonist, someone who started fires for gain of some sort, to a pyromaniac, someone who started fires because they felt some sort of euphoria from doing it. It wasn't like he was going to go around starting fires just for the sake of it, but he had definitely found his go-to method of eliminating threats.

Screams suddenly sounded over the crackling of the flames.

The Canton family was awake and aware of what was going on.

He hoped they died quickly. He didn't wish them ill, he was just doing what he had to do. If the girl had kept her mouth shut, then he wouldn't have had to do this.

As much as he wanted to just stand where he was and soak everything in, committing every second to memory so he could relive it again later in his mind, it wouldn't be long before people started waking and coming out of their houses to watch.

He was just collecting his things and repacking them into his backpack when he heard sirens.

Sirens.

No.

It was too soon.

It had only been about two minutes, three tops since he'd lit the match. They wouldn't be dead yet. He needed more time. How had the fire truck gotten here so quickly?

He had to get out of here.

Last time he had stayed and watched for hours, but this time it would be too risky. With help arriving so quickly, they'd know that he was in the area. He had to leave. Now.

Throwing on his backpack, he didn't bother going back over the fences. That would be too dangerous. Instead, he headed out into the street where people were already beginning to spill out of houses, wrapping robes around themselves and running toward the burning house to see if there was anything they could do to help.

Doing his best to blend in, he sidled into the middle of the road and watched two fire trucks come screeching around the corner.

He couldn't play it cool.

He wasn't going down for this.

He wasn't.

He wouldn't.

He turned and ran.

* * * * *

1:59 A.M.

She was too young to die.

Dakota knew that she should never have gone along with Penny's stupid plan. She had never really wanted to hack into computers and steal tests, but Penny had said it would make them popular and she *so* badly wanted to be popular. She had been sick of always being left out, of being made fun of and teased, of missing out on parties, of being unwanted.

There was nothing wrong with wanting to do all the things other girls her age were doing. She wanted to hang out and talk about boys. She wanted to date boys. She wanted to kiss boys. She didn't want to just think about boys anymore. She didn't deserve to die just for trying to get what everybody else had.

But it looked like she was going to.

"Dakota?" her mother's voice floated through the flames. Her door rattled, but she'd locked it before going to bed. She'd begged for months before finally wearing her parents down and attaining permission to get that lock. Now she couldn't even remember why having her privacy had seemed so important.

Her mother was just outside the door, so close but still so far away. Dakota wanted to get up and go running to her, but she couldn't make herself climb out of bed. Ever since she'd woken up, she'd been hiding under the covers as though they could block out all the bad things in the world just like they had when she was a little girl and scared about something. If her blankets couldn't make things better, then maybe her mom could. Sometimes she said she hated her parents. Sometimes she even believed that she did. They were strict, especially her mom. They didn't understand what it was like to be a kid. They were always focused on her future instead of her present.

Despite all that, she loved them.

So, so much.

And now they were all going to die.

Was this her fault?

Because she and Penny had been so stupid and arrogant to think they could break the law and get away with it?

Or because she'd talked to those cops and told them what had happened?

Maybe the killer had found out she'd talked and was killing her to keep her quiet.

Or maybe this was her punishment for lying.

Or for not being a good enough daughter.

All she wanted was to curl up in her mother's arms and have her make everything better, just like she used to when she was a child.

"Mommy!" she called out. Smoke was already seeping into the room, clogging her throat and making it sore and scratchy.

"Baby? Just hold on; we're coming."

A moment later her door burst open, and her mother and father rushed into her bedroom.

Everything felt like it was moving in slow motion.

It felt like hours had passed since she'd woke to the sound of shattering glass and then crackling flames, but it couldn't have been more than a couple of minutes.

The fire was spreading so fast.

Penny and her family hadn't been able to get out alive. Why would she and her family be any different?

"I love you, sweetheart." Her mother's arms came around her, drawing her close. Dakota snuggled into her mom's embrace. If she was going to die, then at least they were going to die together.

"I'm going for help," her dad announced.

"No," her mom said, sounding panicked. She had never heard her mom panic before. She was the calmest, most even-tempered woman Dakota had ever met.

"I have to." Her dad kissed her forehead, then kissed her mom on the lips and disappeared into the smoky, reddish orange glow.

No sooner had her dad disappeared than she heard sirens.

They were close.

Right outside.

"Baby, come to the window." Her mother took hold of her arms and pulled her from the bed and over to the window.

Just outside there were fire trucks pulled up in the street in front of the house. There was a cop car and an ambulance. There were people milling about everywhere, neighbors and firefighters and police officers, who all seemed to know what they were doing, whether it be as an observer or as someone here to help.

Dakota felt her mind start to get fuzzy.

Help was here, but she didn't seem to know how to get to it.

Thankfully, her mother didn't appear to be having that same problem. She grabbed the bottom of the window and shoved it up.

"Help! Up here!"

Immediately, the attention of everyone outside zeroed in on them.

"Just hold on, sweetheart, they're coming for us." Her mom wrapped her arms around her and held her tightly, kissing the top of her head.

Ever since she'd become a teenager, she had hated her mother's hugs. She'd avoided them whenever she could. They'd felt stifling. Her mother was always so calm. She never argued, no matter how much Dakota provoked her. She had hated that. She'd wanted to see some sort of emotion in the woman who was raising her. Other kids' parents got angry and sad and happy, but not her mom. The only emotion her mom ever showed was irritation. Now she couldn't be gladder of that. Her mom's ability to remain calm no matter what was going to save their lives.

The firefighters were moving a huge ladder toward her second-story bedroom.

It almost seemed too good to be true.

They were so close to being rescued and yet she could hear the flicker of the flames growing closer. Smoke continued to fill the room, and the heat from the fire was almost unbearable.

What if they didn't get here in time?

What if the fire got them first?

How badly did it hurt to get eaten alive by flames?

Would she pass out before they got her?

Those seconds it took the firefighters to get their ladder up to the window seemed like an eternity.

When a guy began to climb up it toward them, it seemed like each rung he climbed took ten times as long as it should have.

He was never going to reach them.

They were going to die.

Dakota felt herself float away.

She was still awake, but it was like she was no longer in her body.

Instead, she was hovering in some distant place far, far away from the fire and the smoke, some place where she was safe.

"Baby, go."

Someone was shaking her.

They were trying to dislodge her from the quiet, peaceful precipice that she was perched on.

She resisted.

Letting her mind drift further away, out of reach of anything and everyone.

"Dakota."

She was shaken more firmly this time, and despite her resistance, they were able to dislodge her and bring her back to her burning bedroom.

"Dakota."

She blinked, and her mom's face came into focus.

A man was there too.

She didn't recognize him, but he was dressed like a firefighter.

"We're going to climb down the ladder," he was saying to her.

Climb?

Down a ladder?

She could barely think, let alone climb.

"Go on, sweetheart." Her mother nudged her toward the open window and the waiting fireman.

She didn't move.

"Dakota." Her mother sounded frustrated.

Part of her relaxed at her mom's irritated tone.

That was the mother that she knew and loved.

Tentatively, she took a step toward the window and looked out. The ground looked a *long* way away. It seemed like such an easy task. Climb through the window onto the ladder, scale down it, reach solid ground, and flee from the inferno her home had turned into.

So simple and yet she still couldn't move.

She could feel her mother's growing agitation, but the firefighter remained unfazed. It was like he had experienced this before. He probably had. Dakota was sure she wasn't the first person to panic being trapped inside a burning building.

"I'm going to put you over my shoulder, carry you down. Okay, Dakota?" the man asked.

Relieved, she nodded. That was much easier than trying to make her body cooperate.

The firefighter leaned in through the window and scooped her up, slinging her over his shoulder.

"Wait," she screeched. "Mom, what about Dad?"

"We'll get your dad out, but you and your mom first." The firefighter's voice vibrated through her body as he spoke.

As he climbed down, she bounced about his body with every step.

His shoulder dug into her stomach and kind of hurt, but she didn't care—anything to get out of that fire.

When they reached the ground, he handed her off to someone, and she was whisked away and deposited in the back of an ambulance. Someone put an oxygen mask on her, and it wasn't until that moment that she realized she was struggling to breathe, wheezing each breath in and out.

The oxygen helped her to breathe easier, but it didn't help her fear.

Her dad was in there.

He'd gone to try to get them help and instead he was going to die.

All because of her.

This was all her fault.

She should have been honest.

Maybe if she had, this wouldn't be happening.

Her mother was beside her, clutching her hand, every bit as scared as she was.

If her dad didn't make it out of there alive, how would she ever face her mother again?

She wanted to go running back in there to find him. If she'd had the energy, maybe she would have tried.

As it was, there was nothing to do but wait.

And wait.

And wait.

Dakota's entire body vibrated with fear.

Her dad was quiet, but he was always supportive of everything she did. He loved her, and she loved him so much. She wished she'd told him more often.

It was taking too long.

If they'd found him, they would be out by now.

It was too late.

Then, by some miracle, she saw a firefighter coming down the ladder with someone slung over their shoulder.

Was it her dad?

Hope ignited inside her.

She didn't fan it until she was sure.

She couldn't face the disappointment.

The firefighter came toward them, still carrying the body, which was loaded onto a stretcher and into the ambulance with her and her mom.

As soon as she saw the face, she burst into tears.

It was her dad.

He was alive.

Somehow, he had survived.

Somehow, they had all survived.

Dakota turned and buried her face in her mother's chest and wept.

* * * * *

2:17 A.M.

The first thing Paige noticed as she pulled into the street was the strong smell of smoke. It was even stronger than it had been at the Oliver house, probably because the Canton house was still ablaze.

The eerie orange glow in the sky held a sense of foreboding. She didn't know yet whether anyone had gotten out alive, but she was praying they did. She and Ryan had made appointments to speak with both Stan Martin, Maya Oliver's ex-boyfriend, and Austin Rupert, Maya's current boyfriend, and Mateo Oliver's biological son. Both of them potentially had the motive to kill the Oliver family, and either of them could have panicked and believed that Dakota Canton had seen something the night of the fire and talked, thus deciding to take her out.

As soon as the 911 call came in that the Canton house was on fire, she'd received a phone call. She'd called her mother and asked her to come and watch the girls so she could get straight there. She was hoping that Dakota knew more than she'd initially told them and was finally ready to talk. Before she'd left, she'd woken Hayley to let her know she had to leave and that Nanna was coming to stay. Yes, it was the middle of the night, and she wanted her daughter to be well rested for school in the morning, but although Hayley had grown to love all her extended family, she was definitely a mommy and daddy's girl. If she'd gotten up in the morning to find neither of them there, she could possibly have a little meltdown.

Paige was parking her car just as she saw her husband with a limp figure slung over his shoulders heading straight for an ambulance. Although he was wearing his helmet, face mask, and self-contained breathing apparatus, she knew it was him. They'd been together for long enough now that she could pick him out anywhere. That he'd carried someone out of the house meant that at least one of the members of the Canton family had to be alive.

Slamming the car door behind her, she jogged toward the ambulance. The body Elias had been carrying was too big to be Dakota or her mother. It had to be the father. Hopefully, the others had already been rescued.

"Elias? You okay?" she asked as she rounded the corner to see him tugging off his SCBA and helmet. As much as she wanted the Canton family to have survived, her husband was the most important person in the world to her, along with their children, and she always worried about him when he had to walk inside a burning building to rescue someone.

"Fine, babe," he assured her, leaning down to give her a quick kiss.

"Did they all make it out?" she asked, nodding her head at the house.

"They did."

"They all alive?"

"The husband was in pretty bad shape by the time we got to him, but yes, they're all alive."

"Dakota able to talk?" It was vital that she talked to the girl as soon as possible. She obviously knew something that had the killer scared enough to set her house on fire to stop her from talking.

"Physically, yes. Psychologically? That's a whole other story. When I found her, the girl was zoned out. She couldn't make it down the ladder. I had to carry her. Maybe now that she's out of the fire, she's safe, and both her parents are also out, she'll be focused enough to answer your questions, but don't be surprised if she can't."

"Okay." At least she was prepared for the possibility of not getting the information she needed tonight.

"How's your head?"

"Better," she assured her husband.

"Still got a headache?"

"It's mostly gone," she replied truthfully, then stood on tiptoe to kiss Elias's cheek. "Here's a kiss from Hayley. She wanted me to give it to you if I saw you before she did."

The smile on her husband's face was one she had felt on her own so many times over the last twelve months. After close to five years of believing that they would never get to be parents, some days raising two little girls still felt surreal.

"Stay safe," she told Elias. The Canton family might be out of the house, but the fire still needed to be extinguished. Her husband's job wasn't over yet.

"You too," he told her, giving her another quick kiss before going off to join his squad.

Paige turned to the ambulance and headed over. Earl Canton lay on a stretcher, wearing an oxygen mask, but he was moving his hands, so she knew that he was doing okay. Sylvia and Dakota sat beside the stretcher, clutching their husband and father's hands. As much as she wanted to let the family relish in being together and alive, she had to go and break up their happy family moment. Right now, Dakota was the biggest key they had to solving this before another fire claimed another family.

"Dakota," she said as she stepped up to the back of the ambulance.

The girl turned large, red-rimmed brown eyes in her direction, and Paige knew immediately that Dakota knew something she hadn't told them.

"We need to talk."

Dakota moved to stand, but her mother snapped a hand around her wrist and held her in place. "Not now, Detective. You can talk to her later. Right now we need to be together."

"Mrs. Canton, your daughter knows something about who set this fire and the fire that killed her friend."

Mrs. Canton looked skeptical but turned to her daughter. "Do you know something you didn't tell them?"

The expression on Dakota's face clearly displayed her answer.

"You answer every question she asks you with complete honesty," Sylvia said firmly.

Dakota nodded meekly and climbed down out of the ambulance. Paige led the girl away from the hubbub surrounding what used to be her home and to a quiet space off to the side. They were blocked by police cars and away from the prying eyes of the neighbors and the reporters who were showing up in ever increasing numbers.

"You lied to us, Dakota," Paige rebuked. "You told us that you and Penny were blackmailing Ian Brownlee because he found out you were hacking teachers' computers to steal and sell tests, but you weren't."

"We *were* stealing the tests," the teenager said in a small voice.

"But Mr. Brownlee never found out about it. You were blackmailing him to get him to break up with Penny's mother because Penny didn't want to see her mother happy." In her years on the police force, she had met a lot of dysfunctional families, but the Oliver family was topping that list. The husband has a secret son, the wife was having an affair, the oldest daughter was dating her father's biological son, and the youngest daughter hated her mother enough to commit blackmail just to sabotage her.

"It was Penny's idea," Dakota said softly.

The girl could try to ascribe blame as much as she wanted, but she had been a willing and active participant in everything that had happened. "We know that you went to Ian Brownlee's house the night Penny and her family were killed. You and Penny were seen standing outside the house talking. Was anyone else there with you? Both of you are too young to have drivers' licenses, so who was your driver?"

"I drove. Penny and I would sneak out sometimes and just go driving around, sometimes in one of her parents' cars, and sometimes in mine."

Since they had no evidence that anyone else was there, Paige would accept that for the moment, then ask Jen Pickles if she could identify the make and model of the car she had seen parked outside the Oliver house shortly before the fire. "You and Penny talked for a bit before you went home. Did you see anyone?"

Dakota hesitated, which clearly said she had.

"What did you see, Dakota? You need to tell me. Whoever it was knows that you saw something. That's why they set your house on fire. They wanted to make sure that you couldn't talk. You and your parents could have been killed. What if he comes back? Tries again? We can keep you safe, but I need to know what you saw because the only way we can completely guarantee your safety is to arrest the arsonist."

"I saw a man," Dakota admitted. "He wasn't old like Mr. Brownlee. He was younger. He was in the bushes near the house. I didn't know what he was going to do. I thought maybe it was just one of Maya's boyfriends. Sometimes she sneaks them in at night."

"Did you get a good look at him? Was he tall, short? Dark skin or light? Brown hair or blond?" Anything that Dakota could tell her would help her with which of their two suspects to focus on.

"I don't know, I swear," Dakota said earnestly. "All I saw was the shadowy figure of a young man. That's it. I promise this time I'm telling you the truth."

Paige wasn't so sure that the teenager was telling all she knew, but she didn't think she was going to get anything else out of her tonight. Dakota seemed to respond better and open up when she was confronted with her lies. Maybe talking to Stan Martin and Austin Rupert would give her the ammunition she needed to finally get the whole truth from Dakota Canton—so far, the only witness they had.

* * * * *

9:33 A.M.

"You think Dakota Canton knows more than she's saying?" Ryan asked his partner as they headed for the interview room. By the time he'd arrived at the scene of the Canton fire, Earl, Sylvia, and Dakota had already left for the hospital. He and his partner had interviewed the neighbors to see if anyone saw anything. A few of them had reported seeing a figure dressed in black running down the street just as the fire trucks showed up, but no one could give them more than that.

"Yes. I'm sure of it. Something in the expression in her eyes when she talks about the night of the Oliver fire. I don't know, I can't explain it exactly, it's just a feeling," Paige replied.

Ryan trusted his partner's feelings as implicitly as he trusted his own. If Paige said she felt that Dakota was hiding something, then he believed the teenager was. "Do you think she knows who the arsonist is?"

Paige pondered that for a moment. "I'm not sure. She knows something, but whether she knows who started the fire, I'm not sure. At best, I think she suspects who it is. I think if she knew for sure, she wouldn't have risked him coming after her and nearly killing her and her family. She was genuinely shaken by the fire. Elias said he had to carry her down the ladder because she was so spaced out she couldn't do it herself. Once we finish up with Stan

Martin and Austin Rupert, we should talk to her again. The gravity of what nearly happened should have sunk in by then, so maybe she'll be more forthcoming. Or we might learn something from one of the guys that we can use to push her into talking."

"If she doesn't talk, the killer could go after her again," he said. He didn't want to see another family killed in such a horrific manner, especially if it could be avoided by Dakota just confessing what she knew and letting them handle things.

"I think she knows that, but you know teenagers aren't always the most logical thinkers."

"Not just teenagers." Ryan had seen more people than he could count make bad decisions and wind up hurt. Ian Brownlee sprung to mind. Instead of admitting the blackmail and the money stealing, he'd tried to kill two cops so he could flee, now he was probably going to be spending the rest of his life behind bars. At least they were both okay. His shoulder hurt, especially if he moved it the wrong way and it pulled on the stitches, and he could tell by the way Paige occasionally rubbed at her temples that she still had a mild headache, but considering how things could have turned out, they were both extremely lucky.

"Can't argue with that."

Ryan opened the door to the interview room where eighteen-year-old Stan Martin was waiting for them. Maya's ex-boyfriend was a popular senior who was the star of the high school football team and who intended to go off to college next year on a football scholarship. From what they'd heard, he hadn't taken Maya breaking up with him very well.

As the door opened, Stan looked up at them with bored blue eyes. Since he was legally an adult, they hadn't needed his parents' permission to speak with him, but his father, a lawyer, had been adamantly against it. Stan, on the other hand, hadn't seemed to care. He'd refused his father's offers to represent him—or to find someone else to do it—and had agreed to come in and answer their questions. Ryan didn't know if it was because he had nothing to hide or because he was so arrogant he thought he could con them.

"Good morning, Mr. Martin," Ryan said as he and Paige took seats at the table.

Stan said nothing.

"Sorry about your loss," Paige said, going the sympathetic route. He and his partner didn't usually play good cop, bad cop, but when they did, they usually switched things up. Today, Paige was going to be the more empathetic one.

"It wasn't my loss," Stan snapped. He might be popular and good at football, but Stan Martin didn't appear to be a very nice human being.

"You and Maya Oliver dated all through your sophomore and junior years. Even if you'd broken up recently, it still has to be hard to lose someone you cared about," Paige pushed.

Stan shrugged. "Things were over between us. What happened to her wasn't any of my business."

"Still, we're not talking about her failing a test or breaking an arm or crashing a car. She was murdered. Someone nailed closed all the doors and then set her house on fire. She and her family were still alive. They knew what was happening, and they fought their way through the smoke and flames to try to escape. They died huddled together on the floor of the kitchen." Ryan watched for Stan's reaction as he gave the blow-by-blow of what the family had endured.

For the first time, there was a flicker of real emotion in the young man's blue eyes. Despite what he said, he still felt something for Maya, and he was affected by her death.

"How did you feel when Maya ended things?" Ryan asked. "Did you try to fight for your relationship?"

"She made it clear there was no point. She had already moved on, got herself a new boyfriend." Stan spat out the last word.

"What about you? Did you move on too?" Paige asked.

"There have been a few girls," Stan said vaguely, and Ryan

assumed he meant he'd been sleeping around but wasn't dating anyone.

"What do you know about Maya's new boyfriend?" Ryan asked.

Stan gave them both an assessing stare. "You already know."

"We'd like to hear it from you."

"She's dating her brother," Stan growled.

"Not technically," Paige corrected. "Mateo may have been Austin's biological father, but he gave up his parental rights, and Austin was legally adopted by his mother's husband. Since in the eyes of the law, Austin is not Mateo's son, and since Maya was adopted and not biologically related to Mateo, then the two aren't siblings."

"Technicalities," Stan said. "They're brother and sister."

Ryan didn't disagree. The relationship was bordering on incest, even if technically it wasn't, it still held the ick factor. "You must have been pretty angry that she dumped you to date her brother."

"Angry and a whole mess of other things." Including hurt, if the look on his face was anything to go by. "Maya and I had a good thing going. We talked about college and starting our lives together; we'd even talked about marriage. She threw it all away just because she hated her father."

Penelope Oliver had blackmailed a teacher because she hated her mother.

And it seemed Maya Oliver had dated her brother because she hated her father.

This family was something else.

The amount of hate that they felt for one another was something he had never seen before, and Ryan wondered where things had gone so wrong. Although everything that had been in the house had been destroyed in the fire, he'd seen photographs of the Olivers when they'd been speaking with family members. In the early years when the girls were small, the family had looked happy. There hadn't been any hint of the animosity that had grown to the point where lies and secrets and betrayals were all that was left. By the end, had they still loved each other? As the smoke and flames closed in around them, did they regret the hostility and hatred that had grown between them? Had they had a chance to lay everything else to rest and be at peace with one another before they died?

Ryan loved his wife and kids more than anything on the planet. He couldn't imagine anything being able to come between them and destroy them. He had an adopted daughter and a biological son, and he loved them both equally. Had the issue of being adopted played into the hatred the girls felt for their parents? No one they had spoken to who knew Mateo had anything bad to say about him, neither did anyone have anything bad to say about Harper, so where had this animosity between the children and their parents come from?

With the family all dead, maybe Maya's partner in crime, Austin Rupert, might be able to give them some answers.

"Stan, where were you the night of the Oliver house fire?" Paige asked.

"Home."

"Is there anyone who can confirm that?"

"My mom works nights."

Short answer, no. "What about last night?" Ryan asked.

"My mom works nights," Stan said again.

With motive and no alibi, Stan Martin was still a suspect.

* * * * *

10:00 A.M.

"He's definitely still in as a suspect," Paige said to Ryan as they closed the door to the interview room Stan Martin was in.

"He had genuine feelings for Maya, and he was hurt by her betrayal. They'd been planning a future, and she threw it away for revenge, but was he angry enough to kill Maya and her entire family?"

"That's the million-dollar question." Paige felt like every time they spoke with someone they uncovered another layer of the Oliver family saga filled with secrets and lies and a dozen more questions they needed to find answers to; but with the family all dead, there was no way to find them.

"Maybe Austin can get us some of those answers. If Maya told her ex-boyfriend that she was dumping him to date someone else for the sole purpose of punishing her father, then maybe she told Austin that too. That and hopefully a whole lot more."

Paige hoped so. She was ready to get some answers and end this case before the killer set another fire and killed someone else. With somewhat waning optimism, she followed her partner into the next interview room where twenty-five-year-old Austin Rupert was waiting for them.

Before the door even closed behind them, Austin looked up at them with anxious brown eyes. "Whatever you need me to do to help you find who killed Maya, I'll do it. Anything. Just name it."

He seemed so sincere, so earnest, that she wondered whether maybe Maya had been using him, and he wasn't a willing participant in her plot to punish her father. "How did you meet Maya?" she asked, interested to find out who had been the instigator in the relationship. If it was Maya and Austin was an unwitting participant, then he probably didn't know anything that could help them. If it had been him, then maybe he was the key to getting the answers they needed.

"I always knew that Robert wasn't my father. I just didn't know who my real father was. All I knew about him was that he didn't want me. He and my mother had been very young when they had me, and he hadn't wanted to be lumbered with the responsibility of a child, so he left. For a while, it was just me and my mom, but when I was four, she got married. Her husband adopted me, but he wasn't a father. I always wanted to know who my real father was, but my mother wouldn't give me a name. It took me years to track down who it was, but about six months ago I finally learned his name. Mateo Oliver."

As hard as it would be to be honest about who her biological parents were, Paige knew that when the time came for Arianna to want to know where and who she came from, she would be honest. She owed her daughter that. She would just have to trust that the love and trust that had been built between them was enough that nothing could ever tear them apart. "How did it go when you met your biological father for the first time?"

"Terrible," Austin said, and his eyes took on a vacant look as though he were lost in thought, perhaps envisioning how he wished that things had turned out.

For Arianna, there would be no reunion with her biological parents. Her father was dead, and her mother was already a part of her life, albeit not as her mother but rather as a sort of older sister or aunt.

"Was Mateo happy to meet you?" Ryan asked.

"No. He told me that I wasn't his son, that he never wanted me, and that he didn't want to see me again."

Those were harsh words, especially from a man who had tried for years to have a biological child with his wife. "That must have hurt," Paige said. They'd looked at both Penelope and Harper as the targets, but there was always the possibility that the true target had been Mateo and that his son had killed him and the rest of his family as revenge for his father wanting nothing to do with him.

"Story of my life."

The way Austin said it was a clear invitation for them to ask why. Paige obliged. "Why?"

"I was abused by my adopted father," Austin told them.

If that were true, and right now they had no reason to doubt that it was, then that was an added reason for Austin to want revenge on his father and the family he had chosen while excluding him.

"I'm sorry that happened to you, Austin," Ryan said. "It must have made you pretty angry to know that your father didn't want you and yet he adopted two girls."

"I know where you're going with that," Austin said. "You're implying that I had a reason to kill him and the family he wanted when he didn't want me, but I didn't set that fire. I didn't need to. I'd already gotten my revenge."

"Maya," Paige said.

"Maya," Austin agreed.

"Were you in love with her?" Ryan asked.

"No. We came to a mutually beneficial arrangement."

"She got to punish her father, and you got to get revenge on him."

Austin nodded.

"But what did Maya want to punish her father for?" Paige asked. She felt like if they could just get a handle on each of the players involved, then they could figure this out.

"Mateo Oliver didn't know how to be a father. He may have thrown me away like I wasn't good enough, but that didn't mean that he treated the daughters he did want as though they were good enough either. He put Maya down all the time, telling her she wasn't good enough, that he wished he hadn't adopted her, that he wished they'd picked a smarter daughter, a nicer daughter, a better daughter. Try being told that pretty much every day of your life since you were old enough to understand what it meant. Mateo didn't deserve me, and he didn't deserve Maya, and when he found out that we were dating, he lost it." Austin had a smug smirk on his face.

Mateo disowned one son, then the daughters he had he didn't seem to like, but how did that play into Danielle Terry being held prisoner in the basement? Paige still couldn't see the connection between the two cases, and yet there had to be one. Someone brought Danielle into that basement, chained her up, tortured and raped her, and left her there. She didn't do that to herself.

"So, you got the desired reaction from your father?" Ryan asked.

"Oh, I got more than that." Austin winked. "Maya and I thought we deserved a little fun after everything that man put us through."

If Austin was the killer, then it made sense that he would have gone after his adopted father as well as his biological father. If he was angry at Mateo for abandoning him and putting him in a situation where he'd been hurt, then he likely would have gone after Robert for hurting him too. At the moment, she was leaning more toward Stan Martin being the killer than Austin.

"Where were you the night of the fire?" Paige asked. For once, she'd like to get an answer that included an alibi. Ian Brownlee was out as a suspect. He'd been in jail when the Canton fire was set. But just because she was currently leaning toward Stan didn't mean Austin was out as a suspect.

Before Austin could answer, her phone began to buzz. Usually, she wouldn't answer it in the middle of interviewing a suspect, but Billy Newton's name was on the screen, and she knew the medical examiner would only be calling if it was something important. Casting a glance at Ryan, she stood and moved to the corner of the room before pressing answer.

"What's up, Billy?" she asked quietly.

"Harper Oliver was two months pregnant," he announced without preamble.

Pregnant?

What were the chances that Harper would be pregnant with a miracle baby and then killed?

Maybe she had been the target.

"Did you run a DNA test to find the father?" she asked.

"I ran all your suspects' DNA against the baby's."

If they knew who the father of Harper's baby was, then hopefully they'd have their killer. "Did you get a hit?"

* * * * *

10:11 P.M.

"Stan."

He looked up when someone said his name and glowered when he saw who it was.

Dakota Canton.

The girl who had very nearly ruined his life.

Thanks to her telling the police what she'd seen the night he'd set fire to the Oliver house, they now considered him a suspect. How well he'd done convincing them otherwise was yet to be determined.

Hiding his anger about Maya dumping him just to punish her father would have been impossible. Everyone knew he hadn't taken the breakup well. He'd trash talked her all over school, started several rumors about the possibility that she really was Mateo and Harper's biological daughter and that she was in an incestuous relationship with her long-lost older brother. There was no way the cops weren't going to find all of that out, so he'd tried to play things angry but disinterested. Like he had already moved on.

Which, in a way, he had.

In fact, in *many* ways, he had.

Dakota being one of them.

"Stan," she said again, taking a tentative step toward him. The girl had the innocent look down pat. It was virtually impossible to stay angry with her. Stan didn't know anyone else like Dakota Canton. She was quiet, shy, self-conscious, lacking in confidence, and yet she was also smart, sweet, funny, and surprisingly good in bed.

Yes, he knew that because they'd slept together a couple of times.

All right, more than a couple.

It was a mistake; he knew that. She was only fourteen and he was eighteen, although his birthday had been only a month ago, and he and Dakota had had sex for the first time right after Maya broke up with him, which was five months before he legally became an adult.

He still wasn't quite sure how it had happened.

He'd been angry, and ironically out running laps of the football field which was what he was doing right now, and she'd shown up. He'd yelled at her to go and that he wanted to be alone right now, and she'd kissed him. Then before he even knew what he was doing, they were both naked and going at it.

Ever since he hadn't been able to stop.

He'd tell her it was over, and he never wanted to see her again.

She'd show up at his house in the middle of the night.

He'd tell her it wasn't going to happen.

She'd kiss him, and they'd wind up in bed.

He'd tell her that was the last time.

She'd show up at his house the following night, and they'd have sex.

It was insanity. He didn't even think he liked her. He was just addicted to her. She was his drug, and like all drugs, she was going to be the death of him.

"I didn't tell them I saw you," Dakota said, twirling her hair around her finger and chewing on her lip in that distracting way she did. Whenever she did it, all he could think about was wanting to feel those lips on a certain appendage of his body.

"You told them something," he growled, shoving aside thoughts of him and Dakota doing it. The cops were already on to him. The last thing he needed was someone seeing him having sex with a fourteen-year-old.

"Not at first," she said earnestly. She took another step closer, apparently feeling the anger inside him and wary of getting too close. "They knew I was there. They asked me why Penny and I were out in the middle of the night. I had to tell them about blackmailing Mr. Brownlee."

Stan knew all about Dakota and Penny's little scheme to get popular and couldn't care less about it. He had way bigger problems to worry about.

That might have been all Dakota said at first, but she'd obviously been pressured to give up more information.

The cops weren't just suspicious of him because Maya had broken up with him. There was more to it than that.

Dakota had said something to put them on his tail.

"Dakota," he said and took a menacing step forward.

She whimpered and backtracked a few steps. She knew he was dark. She knew he was dangerous. She knew he had killed four people in a fire, and she knew he'd set her house on fire, and yet here she was. Alone with him in the dark, at night, on a deserted football field. She might be his addiction, but he was hers.

"They knew I was lying. I don't know how, but they knew. I had to tell them something. I didn't say I saw you there, I swear I didn't. I wouldn't do that to you. I just told them that I saw a young guy hiding in the bushes. I said it was too dark for me to see his face. I didn't tell them I saw you. I didn't. I really didn't," she rambled, then rushed forward and threw herself into his arms.

He wanted to shove her away.

She may as well have given the cops his name.

As angry as he was with her, he didn't shove her away. Instead, he wrapped a hand around her throat and kissed her breathless. "Sometimes I really hate you," he whispered in her ear. He felt her shiver against him and knew it was arousal not fear.

"Dakota, move away. Stan, get down on your knees, hands behind your head."

The voice came out of nowhere, and it took a moment for his head to switch gears from sex to self-preservation.

He could throw Dakota and run, but he didn't know how many cops were out there. They no doubt had guns, and they would no doubt shoot him if they perceived him to be a threat, but Dakota was still in his arms. Maybe he could use her as a human shield. If he had a hostage, they might let him walk out of here.

"Dakota, move away," the voice repeated. It was a female voice. It had to be Detective Hood, who had interviewed him earlier. She was pretty, and if he'd had more time, he might have been able to manipulate her into writing him off as a suspect. He could be very persuasive when it came to beautiful females.

"Dakota, now," a male voice ordered.

So, there were at least two of them. With Dakota as a hostage, he might just be able to make it past two cops.

"No," Dakota said firmly, turning in his arms in the direction the cops' voices were coming from but keeping her body closely pressed against his. "I won't let you hurt him."

"We don't want to hurt him," Detective Hood said. "We want to arrest him." They must have been following Dakota, and she led them straight to him.

"No," Dakota repeated. It seemed he wouldn't have to use her as a hostage if she was willingly using herself as his human shield.

"He killed your best friend and her family," the male cop, Detective Xander, reminded her.

"He tried to kill *you*," Detective Hood added. "Don't let him hurt you again, honey. Move away and let us arrest him."

"No," Dakota said again. "Stan and I love each other."

"He doesn't love you, Dakota. He was sleeping with Penny's mother," Detective Hood informed her.

"I don't believe you," Dakota shrieked.

"Harper Oliver was pregnant with Stan's baby when she died," Detective Hood said.

Dakota's body went perfectly still, and he could feel the chill radiate off her as the cop's words sunk in. "No," she said softly.

"Yes, I'm sorry," Detective Xander confirmed.

She was going to move away from him. Stan could feel it. He couldn't let that happen. He needed her to walk out of here alive.

It seemed like whichever route you took with a woman, you ended up burned. You got invested in the relationship and planned a future together, and they dumped you; you tried keeping things purely physical, and they wanted more. Sex with Harper and Dakota had been just that. Sex. Yet both had read more into it than that.

When she'd told him she was pregnant and asked him to raise her miracle baby together, he'd said no. He didn't want a kid. He wanted to go to college on a football scholarship, then go pro. He wasn't going to be tied down. Unfortunately, Harper hadn't taken his rejection well. She'd announced she was divorcing her husband, and since he was a legal adult at the time of their relationship, she had nothing to be ashamed of and was going to have him named as the baby's father and have him support her and their baby.

He wasn't about to be blackmailed.

He didn't want to give up football to get a job and support some kid he didn't even want.

Harper thought she could blackmail him into being with her.

Maya had thrown him away for a chance at revenge.

And suddenly the notion of getting some revenge of his own had been very appealing.

Take them both out, as well as the baby, in one fell swoop. As a bonus, he could frame that idiot Ian Brownlee who actually believed that the affair he was having with Harper meant something to her. She hated her husband and wanted to sleep around. That was as deep as it had been. But then Penny and Dakota had been right outside the house enacting their own little revenge scheme, and it had been perfect. It would lead the cops right to Ian, and it had. At first, at least. Only somehow the man had managed to be so stupid as to get himself caught.

Well, he wasn't about to make that same mistake.

Dakota was going to obey the cops' orders and move away from him.

Pulling a knife from his pocket, he pressed it against Dakota's neck, deep enough to draw blood.

"We're walking out of here. You try to stop us, I kill her," he threatened.

"You kill her, you lose your leverage," Detective Hood countered.

She was right.

There had to be a better way to leverage his hostage.

And he knew just what it was.

"You lower your weapons and let us walk away, or I start slicing off bits of her, maybe a finger first, or an ear, maybe her nose. Her screams will soon change your minds." Cops were do-gooders. They wanted to save people; they couldn't just stand by and listen to Dakota's screams of pain as he mutilated her.

"Put the knife down, Stan. It's over. You're not walking out of here a free man. Don't make things worse for yourself," Detective Hood attempted to reason with him.

Make things worse for himself?

How could he possibly do that?

They already had him on the arson and four counts of murder, plus three of attempted murder. Cutting off a few pieces of Dakota wasn't going to add any additional years to his prison sentence. He could only live so long, and there weren't enough years to punish him for everything he'd already done.

He wasn't going to stand here and discuss it and wait for more cops to show up. He had to get out of here—the quicker, the better. Once he got to his car, he'd just drive and not stop. Maybe he'd bring Dakota along for the ride. It could be fun having her with him to take care of his needs, and if she turned out to be more trouble than she was worth, he could always dump her body along the way.

Stan moved the knife to Dakota's right hand, slicing it through her pinkie finger.

As soon as he did, someone slammed into him from behind.

He'd played his cards and lost.

They'd tricked him.

While Detective Hood had been talking to him and keeping his attention focused on her, her partner must have circled around to get him from behind the moment the knife was away from Dakota's neck.

He'd lost.

He had killed Maya and Harper as karma for what they'd done to him, and now that same karma had circled back around to get him for the bad things he'd done.

Life sucked.

* * * * *

11:28 P.M.

He couldn't be happier to be on his own.

It was nice not to have to worry about a partner. He certainly wasn't missing it at all.

This was the way to do things.

He'd always been a loner. He was comfortable by himself; people were untrustworthy, so it saved a lot of time and heartache to rely on yourself and yourself alone.

Working with a partner had been necessary for the first stage. He wasn't sure things would have gone as smoothly had he done it on his own, but that was over with now. From here on out, he didn't need anyone's help.

Opening the door to his specially created little room, he couldn't contain his glee.

Glee.

It wasn't a feeling he was used to.

It wasn't a feeling he'd had much experience with.

Life for him hadn't been good. He'd suffered a lot, and now it was time to turn the tables on life. He wasn't going to be the victim anymore. From here on out, he was going to be the one in control. He was going to be the one inflicting pain and suffering. Maybe that would help him to finally move on.

Was it wrong for him to inflict suffering on others, knowing what it was like to have it inflicted on himself?

Possibly.

Did he care?

No.

He was done with caring. He was done with being a good human being. That got you nowhere in life, so why should he bother? He should take care of himself and do what made him happy. If anyone ever deserved some happiness, it was him. He had done the bad in life—in spades—and now it was time to experience the good.

His victim was right where he'd left her.

Not that she could really have been anywhere else, he chortled to himself, since he'd left her chained to the ceiling.

Amy hung limply in her chains, her entire weight hanging off her wrists that were shackled to the chains that hung from the ceiling. Her chin rested against her chest, and she didn't indicate that she was aware he had entered the room.

He wasn't worried though.

He had calculated how long she could last without water, and they hadn't yet reached that limit. He was always *very* meticulous. It had served him well throughout every other aspect of his life, and he knew it would serve him well in this new venture. It hadn't been safe for him to make many journeys here to visit her, so he'd had to leave her and trust that the research he had done would hold.

Unscrewing the cap to a bottle of water, he closed and locked the door behind him and carried the water to Amy. He fisted her hair and tilted her head back, ripping off the gag so he could dribble some water down her throat.

Almost immediately, he noticed a change in her. She started to stir as the water rehydrated her body. He didn't want her too hydrated. He wasn't in the mood for a battle. He was tired after the stresses of the last few days, and he just wanted to have a little fun, then go and get some much-needed sleep.

He unlocked the cuffs around her wrists and caught Amy as she dropped. She moaned in agony as blood flow resumed to her deadened limbs. The sound of her pain was like an aphrodisiac, and he needed to cause her more to feed his desires. It was a need; he'd never felt anything like it before. He'd always been attuned to pain, but usually, it was his own. To feel someone else's was like nothing he'd ever experienced. It was a high he was never going to get tired of experiencing.

Gathering the young woman into his arms, he carried her over to his specially prepared table. The more aware she became, the more panicked she was. She was starting to fight him now, albeit fairly pathetically. Without the gag, she was capable of talking, but her mouth seemed to be as numb as her arms, and all she was uttering was a string of unintelligible ramblings.

Laying her out on the table, he snapped her wrists and ankles into the leather cuffs and secured them firmly. He was going to need her to remain still for what he was about to do.

He wasn't completely cold and unfeeling.

Yet.

He'd do Amy one last little favor.

Reaching up, he undid the blindfold and let it fall away.

Amy blinked, her eyes struggling to remain open as her pupils dilated in the sudden light that she had become unaccustomed to.

He waited until her vision cleared. He knew that she knew who he was, but he wanted to give her one last chance to see him before he permanently stole her sense of sight. He owed her that much, at least. Probably more, but that was the best he could give her right now.

When she was able to keep her eyes open, they met his, and the two locked together. She was begging him to let her go. He could read it in her eyes. He could feel it inside him. He should feel some sort of compassion for her. He was, after all, the one responsible for her current predicament and for what was to come.

But he didn't.

He had crossed over some invisible bridge from normal, sane human, to a vicious monster.

There was no going back.

He wasn't even sure that he wanted to go back.

He was happy.

For the first time in his life, he was really and truly happy.

He reached into the drawer just under the table and pulled out a needle and thread. Amy's eyes grew wide when she saw them. She knew what was coming.

"No, please," she murmured.

It was too late for pleas.

This was what he *wanted* to do.

"Be a good girl and don't fight me," he told her. He would knock her out if he had to, but he didn't want to. He wanted to feed off her suffering. He wanted to ride this high and then come inside her so hard he forgot his own name.

Threading the needle, he took her lip between his fingers and pressed the tip through her flesh. This night was going to be one he'd never forget.

* * * * *

11:59 P.M.

Watching her baby daughter sleep was something Paige never tired of doing.

In the blue glow of the nightlight, Arianna looked so peaceful. She was lying on her stomach, her lips parted in a small o, one hand curled around her favorite toy—her stuffed rabbit.

Whenever Paige looked at her daughters, part of her wanted them to stay this little forever. She didn't want them to grow up and move away. She wanted to hold on to them and never let them go. But at the same time, she loved watching her girls grow and learn new things. Every time she saw Hayley try something new and achieve it, she felt so proud, and watching Ari learn to sit and crawl and try to walk and talk, there was nothing that beat that.

It had been a rough couple of days.

The Oliver case had really rocked her.

Seeing what a mess they had made of their family was making her think about her own family.

What if the same thing happened to them?

What if one day she woke up and her two beautiful little girls hated her?

What if she woke up one day to find that the love between her and her husband had died?

She couldn't imagine that happening, but ten years ago, had Mateo and Harper imagined that this was what would become of them and their children?

Carefully, she reached into the crib and slid her hands under Arianna and scooped her up, cradling her in her arms and going to sit in the rocking chair. Ari stirred a little but almost immediately snuggled back down. Her baby girl was almost too big for nighttime cuddles like this. When the girls had first come to live with them and everything that had happened with her stalker had still been so fresh that getting through each day was a struggle, at night when she couldn't sleep, she'd come into the nursery and sit in the rocking chair holding her baby and rock them both until her overwhelming fears calmed to a manageable level.

"Can't sleep, babe?"

Paige looked up to see Elias standing in the nursery doorway. "Nope."

He came over and picked her up, then settled in the rocking chair with her and Arianna on his lap. As Elias rocked all three of them, Paige stroked Arianna's silky soft little head. How would she cope if this beautiful, sweet little baby girl turned around one day and told her that she hated her?

She wouldn't.

Her family was her life.

She couldn't lose them.

"We're not the Oliver family," Elias said softly in her ear.

Paige knew that.

She did.

She really did.

Any yet, it didn't seem to help her let go of the doubts.

Maybe it was because she doubted herself. Her life had been messed up in the worst possible way. She'd been robbed of her ability to have children of her own; she'd feared—truly feared—that she would lose her life; she'd been violated, and some of what had happened had been her fault because she had underestimated her stalker. Part of her felt like she didn't deserve two amazing children.

"I hate when you think that way." Her husband began to rub soothing circles on her back. He knew the motion always helped to calm her when she was anxious.

"I can't help it."

"What happened with your stalker wasn't your fault. You don't deserve to be punished for something that was outside your control."

Logically, she knew that he was right, but it was hard when your head and your heart weren't on the same page. "Dakota might lose her finger," she said. "She's in surgery; they're hopeful that they'll be able to reattach it, but there are no guarantees. Even if the surgery is successful, she has a really long road ahead of her both physically and psychologically."

"She made her choices."

She had.

Dakota had believed that she was in love with Stan. She'd believed that he loved her back. She hadn't known that he was sleeping around with other women, including her best friend's mother.

The whole thing was just crazy.

A break up and an unwanted baby had caused four people to die in such a horrific manner.

It wasn't worth it.

There were so many other ways things could have happened.

If the Oliver family had been a united front, then the wheels that set all of this into motion would never have been turned.

It all boiled down to the adoption.

If Mateo and Harper had been able to have children of their own, then none of this would ever have happened.

"It's the adoptions," she said softly, reflexively holding her baby closer.

"No," Elias said firmly.

"Dakota told me why Penny hated her mother." Dakota had been hysterical while Paige kept the pressure on her wound as they waited for the ambulance to arrive and had spilled everything about Penny, Stan, and the entire situation. "It was because Harper was always telling her that she wasn't pretty enough, that she wasn't popular enough. She was always pushing makeup and clothes at her as though her appearance was the only thing that mattered. She actually told Penny that it was too bad she wasn't her biological daughter because if she were, she would have inherited her genes." Paige couldn't imagine saying something like that to her daughters. They may not have grown inside her, but they were a part of her in a way that could never be changed. But could it be broken?

"Paige, you have to let this go. We're not them; they're not us. The things that Harper said to Penny were terrible; the things Mateo said to Maya were terrible, but can you imagine us saying things like that to our children?"

She shook her head.

"Right. We don't care that Hayley and Ari are adopted, we don't love them less because of it, and we couldn't love them more if they were biologically ours. Not being able to have kids didn't tear us apart. It brought us closer. When we look at our girls, we see our girls, and when we see each other, we see our other half."

Her husband was being particularly corny tonight, and she loved him for it. It was exactly what she needed. Elias had been right there beside her during the darkest days of her life. He hadn't backed away—not even for a second. He'd held her at night while she was plagued by nightmares and during the day when she suffered panic attacks. He'd helped her grow strong again. She could never repay him for everything he'd done for her.

At first, after she'd learned that she could no longer get pregnant, she had tried to push him away, told him that she understood if he wanted to divorce her and find someone else who could give him the children he deserved.

Elias had promptly shut that down.

"Each and every member of the Oliver family contributed to it falling apart. That doesn't mean that they deserved what happened to them; they didn't—no one deserved that, but they were all responsible for letting things get to the point where they all hated one another."

"You don't think that will ever happen to us?" Paige asked. She knew in her heart that it wouldn't, but she needed a little reassurance right now.

"I know it won't," he answered confidently and pressed a kiss to her temple.

He was right. They loved each other too much to ever let hate get a foothold in their family. Would things always be easy with the girls or each other? No. They would face stresses and anxieties and hard times just like every other family. The girls would get older, go through teenage dramas. There would be the inevitable issues that arose in any marriage, but her family was strong enough to weather it all.

"Ready to go to bed now?" Elias asked.

"Yes. Why don't you go and get Hayley and the girls can sleep with us tonight." She just needed to feel close to them right now. She wanted to fall asleep with her husband's arms around her and their girls between them. Usually, they only had sleepovers in their huge king size bed for something special like family days, but to her, this was one of those special occasions. What could be more special than celebrating family?

OCTOBER 31ST

"Dakota Canton's surgery was successful," Paige announced as she set her cell phone down on her desk. "Barring any infections, with some physical therapy and time, she'll regain full use of her finger."

"I think the physical recovery is going to be a whole lot easier than the psychological recovery," Ryan said.

She agreed wholeheartedly. "You think she knew what he was going to do that night?"

"No. I don't think she really knew who Stan Martin was. To her, he was just an older, popular football player who all the girls at her school dreamed about dating and she had him. Part of him, at least."

"She was willing to die for him." Suspicious of Dakota and convinced the teenager knew more than she was saying, they had sat outside the hotel where the Canton family was staying, waiting to see what the girl would do. They hadn't had to wait long. After about fifteen minutes, they'd seen her sneaking out. They'd followed her to the high school football field where they'd listened to Stan all but admit that he was the killer. Instead of listening to them and moving out of the way so they could arrest Stan, she had stood right in front of him, blocking them and preventing them from being able to take him down.

"Only until she learned who the real Stan was."

Dakota had appeared ready to remove herself as Stan's human shield once they told her about Harper Oliver's pregnancy. Before she could, Stan had pulled the knife and held it to her throat.

Things had come very close to having a very bad ending. If she hadn't been able to keep Stan distracted while Ryan got into position, then Sylvia and Earl Canton would be planning their daughter's funeral.

"Stan Martin is in jail where he belongs. He's no longer a danger to Dakota or anyone else," Ryan said. "Hopefully her parents will get her the psychological help she needs to come to terms with everything that happened. And now we can focus on closing the Danielle Terry case."

"I still haven't been able to locate the friend, Amy. I've contacted every school in the area including the private schools, but none of them have a girl named Amy who matches our description. I also contacted Danielle's social worker and asked her if there were any Amys who'd been with her in any of the foster homes she'd spent time in, but there weren't."

"Did you sleep at all last night?" Ryan asked with a one-sided smile.

"I did." She had—more peacefully than she had in months. Hayley had been groggily excited when Elias brought her to sleep in their bed, and with her husband and her girls by her side, she had slept deeply and contentedly. "Ari decided she wanted to get up at five, so I finished Hayley's costume, got a start on dinner, did two loads of laundry, and started making phone calls at seven. I lucked out and was able to speak with the social worker and the schools before I had to leave to get here."

"You're a busy bee today," he said, parroting his six-year-old daughter's favorite phrase.

Paige laughed. Hayley had started saying that too. She was like a little sponge. She sat back and watched and listened, often picking up sayings from her best friend, Sophie. She sobered as she thought of Danielle Terry's naked body hanging in that basement, raped, mutilated, and left to die alone and scared. "We need to find proof it was Mateo. I know he's dead, and we can't prosecute him, but Danielle deserves justice, and her foster mother Sally deserves closure."

"And we need to find where he stashed Amy."

"You think she's a victim too?"

"Don't you?" Ryan asked.

"Yes. But who is she? How are we going to find her if we can't even find out who she is?"

"Simple answer would be that Danielle's friend's name wasn't really Amy."

"If they didn't want Sally to know who she was for some reason, then they might have lied about her name," Paige agreed. It made as much sense as anything else, especially if the girls were already planning to run away.

"If we start with the girls in Danielle's class, we should get Sally Shield to look through class photos and see if she can identify the girl who she saw talking with Danielle."

"I went through missing persons and there wasn't anyone who I thought could be a match for Amy, either under the name Amy or through their descriptions."

"You really were busy this morning."

"I can't stand the thought of this girl out there all alone and scared and praying someone finds her."

"She might already be dead." Ryan voiced the fear she'd been unable to let herself think about. "He didn't leave Danielle in good shape. Even if the smoke from the fire hadn't killed her, she didn't have long left. Assuming he took both girls at the same time and assuming he did the same things to both, then Amy—or whoever she is—could already be dead from dehydration, blood loss, or septic shock."

Her partner was right.

She knew that.

But she wasn't ready to give up on Amy just yet. If the girl was still alive, then she was counting on them to find her.

Before Paige could say anything else, Stephanie Cantini came rushing up to their desks. The forty-five-year-old crime scene tech looked breathless like she'd run the entire way from the lab to their desks. Stephanie was a good friend and another member of the adopted family club. Well, not that there was a club, but Stephanie was single and had an adopted daughter, Cindy, who was now eighteen, who she'd raised on her own. Paige wondered whether all parents of adopted kids were concerned if one day their child would throw it back in their face that they weren't their "real" parent. She was going to have to get a handle on these worries and anxieties before they grew and got in the way of her ability to be the mother Hayley and Arianna deserved. Maybe she'd speak with Charlie Abbott about it. He'd been her therapist after she'd been raped and nearly murdered and been a godsend. Maybe he could help her with this as well. She made a mental note to call him.

Paige didn't even have to ask if it was good news from the way Stephanie's hazel eyes were twinkling. Whatever she had for them was case breaking, or at the very least, case cracking. "What did you find, Steph?"

"DNA." Stephanie beamed.

"DNA?" Ryan echoed. "On who?"

"On your girl in the basement. Danielle Terry. Billy was able to find some under her fingernails. The girl fought her attacker, managed to get in at least a few good scratches. There was enough there for me to get a good sample and run it through the sequencer."

"And you got a match?" Paige asked.

"Yep." Stephanie's beam grew bigger.

"Mateo?" Ryan asked.

"Nope."

No?

If Mateo Oliver hadn't been the one to abduct, rape, and mutilate Danielle Terry, then who was? And how had they managed to get her into the Oliver house unseen? And how had no one in the Oliver house noticed she was there?

Before her mind could spin off in a million different directions, seeking answers to each new question that popped into her head, she asked, "Then who did it match? Harper or one of the girls?" Although female sexual offenders were rare, it wasn't impossible that Danielle's attacker had been female. You didn't need to have a penis to sexually assault someone.

"Close. It wasn't Harper or Maya or Penelope, but it was a family member."

There was only one biological relative of Mateo they knew about.

And they already knew that he hated Mateo and was out for revenge.

Austin Rupert.

* * * * *

10:42 A.M.

"Thank you for meeting with us at such short notice," Ryan told Lesley and Robert Rupert as they led him and Paige through their house and into the kitchen.

"Of course," Lesley said as she indicated that they should take a seat at the large round kitchen table.

From the moment the couple had opened the door—hand in hand—they had seemed resigned, as though they had always expected this day to come. Ryan wondered what the couple knew about their son that he and Paige didn't. Had they known that Austin was capable of what he'd done to Danielle Terry and her friend? If they had, then why hadn't they done something to stop it from happening?

"We need to talk to you about your son," Ryan announced once they were all seated, and the couple visibly braced themselves. Robert reached out to take his wife's hand. Whatever was coming, they were clearly in this together.

"What can you tell us about him?" Paige asked.

The couple exchanged glances, and Lesley gave Robert a small nod. The man met their gaze squarely, and said, "Austin has a lot of problems."

According to Austin, his adoptive father had been abusive. That wasn't the vibe Ryan was getting from the man, but some people were better at hiding their true self than others. If Austin had been abused, it could have been the catalyst for his current behavior, or the story could have been a lie devised to help procure their sympathies should they begin to seriously consider him a suspect in the fires.

"Austin said you abused him, Mr. Rupert." Paige confronted the man calmly.

Robert nodded, his gaze didn't drop, and he didn't appear either surprised or defensive about the accusation. Lesley let out a small cry and leaned closer in toward her husband, not the behavior you might suspect from a man who had abused her son.

"Austin would hurt himself," Robert explained.

That wasn't a unique story. He and Paige had interviewed several abusive parents who claimed either the injuries their children suffered were nothing more than unfortunate accidents or that the children had inflicted the injuries upon themselves.

For the first time, Ryan believed it might be true in this instance.

"He used to throw himself off the top bunk or down the stairs to cause bruises and broken bones. He would get into the medicine cabinet and take whatever he could find in there to make himself ill. He would take my shoes and my belt and hit himself with them to make it look like I hurt him," Robert said.

"Or you hit him with your shoes or your belt, leaving him with bruises. You broke his bones and gave him your medications to make him sick," Paige said.

"He started doing it before I even met Robert," Lesley said softly. "He was two the first time he did it. He picked up a fork and stuck it into his arm. At first, I just thought it was normal child behavior, I was just a kid myself when I had him. I didn't know anything about raising children. I thought it was just him learning about pain. But then he kept doing things, and I knew something was wrong. I just didn't want to believe it."

If Austin had been getting hurt in atypical ways before his mother was married, perhaps she was the abuser.

"I know what you're thinking." Robert glowered at them and wrapped a protective arm around his wife's shoulders. "But child protective services already investigated. When Austin kept taking time off school for injuries or illnesses, and when he did show up, he always had new bruises or cuts and scrapes, the school reported us. Austin was removed from the home, and we were both interviewed at length. They cleared us when examination of Austin's injuries proved that they were self-inflicted. The angles of some of the bruises he inflicted by hitting himself could only have been made if he'd done it himself. We were cleared, but we were told to get him some mental health care. Which we did. He was diagnosed with Munchausen Syndrome when he was nine."

People with Munchausen Syndrome deliberately made themselves ill, tried to mimic a disease or falsified trauma to gain attention and sympathy. Austin's behavior certainly seemed to fit that diagnosis.

"We sent him to a therapist," Lesley said, a couple of tears rolling slowly down her cheeks. "We tried to get him help, but nothing seemed to work. We were so afraid, we didn't know what to do. We even had him committed, but he was so smart, and he knew how to play the system. He would pretend that he was getting better and they would let him out. For a time, things would improve, and we'd get our hopes up that maybe he really was getting better, but then he'd start again."

"It was heartbreaking," Robert said. "To see that boy, who I thought of as my own son, hurt himself and no matter what you did, you couldn't get it to stop. By the time he was twelve, he'd started showing a violent streak toward others. We have a daughter. She's five years younger than Austin, and she soon became the target of his attention."

The ominous way the man said it made it clear exactly what kind of attention Austin had showered on his little sister.

"We made sure that they were never alone together," Lesley said. "But he was so quick. He'd wait for that split second when you went to the bathroom or took a shower or went to check on food on the stove, and then he'd pounce on her. We had to start having her sleep in our room at night because he would wait until we were asleep and then go into her room and hurt her."

"It got to the point where it didn't even matter if we were in the room, he'd hurt her anyway, and there was nothing we could do about it. At twelve, he was too big for me to handle physically," Robert said.

"You're not a small man, Mr. Rupert," Paige said.

"No, I'm not, but Austin was a big boy, and when he got in one of his moods, it was like he became supernaturally strong. He would torture his sister relentlessly. Not always physically. He liked to mentally torture her too. One day he locked her in this little cage he made in the basement. I was only gone from the room for two minutes, but that was all it took for him to whisk her away. It took us over four hours to find them. It was the middle of summer, over one hundred degrees, and by the time we found her, she was almost dead. She'd ripped her fingernails out trying to claw her way out, and that was when we knew. We had no choice. We had to send him away."

"We didn't want to." Lesley began to cry in earnest now. "He was our son, we loved him, but we couldn't control him. Therapy wasn't working, and we had to do whatever we could to protect our daughter. When he was fourteen, he went to live in a group home for troubled teens, and when he turned sixteen, he became emancipated. I haven't spoken to him since the day they came to take him away." Lesley turned and buried her face in her husband's shoulder.

Robert patted her back as he spoke. "He disowned us. We've tried more times than I can count to reach out to him, try to make amends. We knew there was something wrong with him, we just didn't know how to fix it. What has he done?"

"We believe that he abducted two teenage girls with the idea of setting his biological father up for the crimes. He put one of them in Mateo's basement. Presumably, he thought sooner or later Mateo's wife or daughters would find her and turn him into the cops. We're trying to find where he's put the other girl. I know you said you haven't spoken to him since he was fourteen, but do you have any idea of where he might hide her?" It seemed like a long shot if it had been eleven years since they'd last seen their son, but right now it was the best chance they had at finding the other girl before it was too late.

"I don't know," Robert said, looking devastated at the news of what the young man he considered a son had done. "I'm sorry. I wish I could help, but I have no idea where he'd hide this poor girl."

"His sister might." Lesley lifted her tearstained face. "It didn't matter how many times he hurt her, she never stopped worshipping him. They've maintained a relationship of sorts. I'll get you Amy's contact information."

Amy?

What were the chances that Sally Shield had seen her foster daughter talking with an Amy shortly before she ran away and ended up chained up in a basement tortured and raped and that Amy wasn't Austin's sister and the only person he appeared to be close to?

None.

But was Amy still working with her brother or had she found herself his latest victim?

* * * * *

12:06 P.M.

To know that her own brother was responsible for her current predicament was a bitter pill to swallow.

To know that she had given him the opportunity to do this to her was an even worse pill to take.

Amy had walked like a lamb to the slaughter right into Austin's trap.

Now she had to pay the price for her stupidity.

And that price would be steep.

Her brother obviously intended to keep her here, wherever here was, for a long time. He'd moved her from the chains to a table. It was padded and would have been comfortable to lie on if she hadn't already been lying on it for hours on end. He'd put a feeding tube down her nose and an IV in her arm. He'd even inserted a catheter, whatever he had planned, he wanted to make sure she was alive to experience it.

She probably could have handled all of that if it wasn't for what else he'd done.

She couldn't stop thinking about it.

It didn't help that giving her painkillers hadn't been on his to do list, so she couldn't *not* think about it even if she wanted to.

It hurt.

It hurt so bad, it took all her willpower not to burst into a fit of tears. If she cried, then her nose would get all stuffed up, and since he'd sewn her mouth closed and she could no longer breathe through it, if she couldn't breathe through her nose then she'd suffocate.

Maybe that was a better option.

Amy had thought she was dead already. She'd already passed out before Austin returned. She'd made her peace with life and death and been ready to pass on. But now she was back to endure a possibly unending amount of suffering.

She wished she'd died.

Anything had to be better than this.

A sob almost escaped.

She wanted to see. It was terrifying having her eyes sewed closed, besides the pain and the pulling on the stitches every time her eyes tried to blink, or she subconsciously tried to open them. Being trapped in the darkness was petrifying. Amy had been scared—terrified—of the dark ever since she was a very little girl. Because the dark was when her brother would come for her. Austin had haunted her nights for as long as she could remember, making her both frightened and oddly comforted.

There was something wrong with her.

How could her brother's torturous behavior comfort her?

How could it make her feel safe?

Why didn't she hate him?

Why did she insist on continuing their dysfunctional relationship?

Why did she let him control her?

What power did he have over her?

It was like some sort of weird Stockholm Syndrome, battered wife type situation. The more she knew he was going to hurt her and that she should stay away from him, the more she was drawn to him. It was like he cast a spell over her and she couldn't think clearly.

Normally, she was a smart woman. She was studying business management in college. She wanted to build her own business—a chain of interior design stores selling everything from linens to wall art to vases and everything in between. There were so many things she wanted to do with her life, and none of them included helping her brother kidnap some foster kid nobody would care about just so he could set up his biological father.

It was insane.

She was insane.

How could she let this happen?

What was wrong with her?

She wanted to scream and rant and rave, but he'd robbed her of that as well. Why did he hate her so much? Amy had never known the answer to that question. She didn't understand what she had done to make her the center of his hatred and anger. She'd been just a child the first time he'd hurt her. She couldn't have done anything to make him hate her that badly.

Fear.

Her fear was a real thing, a living thing. It moved through her bloodstream, leaving no part of her untouched. It flowed around her, never stopping, never letting up. It was just always there. Sometimes it hit her heart, making it race so fast it felt like it was going to run right out of her chest—and sometimes it flooded her throat, choking her. And sometimes it reached her limbs, hitting them so hard it made them shake uncontrollably.

She wanted a break from it.

Just a moment to rest and regather her strength.

But it was there.

Always there.

Someone was coming.

She sensed it even before she heard the footsteps or the key sliding into the lock.

Austin was back.

What was he going to do to her?

Earlier she'd been afraid that he was going to rape her, but he hadn't. He'd raped that homeless girl. Violently. That was something she wished she hadn't seen. She'd wanted to leave, but Austin had insisted that she stay; he could be so sadistic. She should never have let him convince her to pretend to be an abused foster kid to con that girl into coming with her. She was so stupid. Right about now she would gladly go to prison if she could just get her sight back and her mouth back and get out of this room.

"Lunchtime, sister," Austin sang as he entered the room.

How could she eat lunch? He'd sewn her lips together, maybe so she couldn't scream for help, but she supposed it was more because he just wanted to make her suffer. Austin lived for suffering, his own or someone else's. It never used to matter to him, but now he seemed to have developed a liking for other people's suffering.

She felt fiddling with her feeding tube. It tugged all the way through her nose and down her throat. It felt weird. Her whole body felt weird. There were too many foreign things inside of her. The threads, the tubes, the catheters—she just wanted them all gone. Amy had no idea how Austin had learned all of these medical things, putting in stitches and tubes and IVs. As far as she had known, these were all skills he didn't possess, but he'd spent a lot of time in hospitals growing up, and he'd obviously learned a lot. Or, perhaps more terrifyingly, he had learned how to do these things with this plan in mind, which meant he had always intended to bring her here and keep her as his prisoner.

Austin fiddled with the table, and she was propped up into a sitting position, then she heard him walking about doing who knows what.

Amy wished she could know what her brother was doing, what he had in this room, what was on his face and in his eyes. How did she stand a chance at convincing him to let her go when she had no tools at her disposal? She was restrained, she couldn't speak, and she couldn't see.

Not being able to see was the worst.

It wasn't the pain. It was the fear of not knowing what was coming, of being compromised and vulnerable.

"Quiet today, aren't you?" Her brother laughed at his own joke. He was really getting off on what he was doing to her. If he was this cruel already, what was it going to be like in a few days? Or a few weeks? Or months? How long could she live like this? He was making sure she was kept hydrated and making sure her body was getting the nutrition that it needed. Did that mean he could keep her alive indefinitely?

That was a terrifying prospect.

How would she cope?

She wouldn't.

Amy wanted to wrap her hands around her evil brother's neck and squeeze and squeeze until she squeezed the life right out of him.

Subconsciously, her hands curled into fists.

Austin noticed and laughed like it was the funniest thing he'd ever seen. "You know, Amy, we're not so different, you and I. I just admit who I am, and you try to hide it."

He was wrong.

She wasn't anything like Austin.

Her brother was evil.

Pure evil.

He was like a lion playing with its prey.

And she was the prey.

* * * * *

12:40 P.M.

"What would possess Amy Rupert to go along with her brother's plan?" Paige didn't understand what had been going through the young woman's head when she'd let her brother talk her into helping him.

From all accounts, Amy appeared to be a bright young woman. She had graduated high school with a 4.0 grade point average, she was top of her class at college, she was well liked by her friends, and she worked part-time as a receptionist at a dentist office where she was both liked and respected by colleagues and patients. She'd had her whole life ahead of her and yet she had thrown it away to help her brother. If she wasn't dead already, then she would be spending the rest of her life in prison as an accomplice in the abduction, rape, torture, and death of Danielle Terry.

"Years of abuse, not just physical, but mental and emotional as well, messed with her head," Ryan said. "In a way, Austin's abuse was a constant. It was something stable that she could depend on always happening. I guess to Amy it became a sort of comfort. She loved him, despite everything he did to her, and because he was such a dominant force in her life, he was able to convince her to help him."

"He played with her emotions, I guess. Made her feel sorry for him. He seemed to be good at that." From what they had learned, manipulating people was basically how Austin Rupert made his living. He gambled a little, mostly poker, and appeared to be able to read people well enough that most of the time he won. He didn't have a house of his own but bounced around from friend to friend, all of whom seemed okay with opening up their home to him.

"He's a smart guy, and he's been playing games his whole life, manipulating people. He knows what he's doing, and he's dangerous. We need to be careful," Ryan said as Paige parked the car in front of Amy Rupert's house.

The house was quite large, a modern rectangular building mainly black painted concrete and huge glass windows. It was a nice neighborhood, and Paige wondered how a college student who worked part-time had been able to afford a house like this. It wasn't a rental, she owned it. Well, she had a mortgage on it.

"Think Austin gave her the money for the house?" she asked as she climbed out of the car.

"Probably. Could be one of the ways he was able to manipulate her into helping him."

Her partner was probably right. A combination of threatening to hurt her, years of conditioning through abuse, and reminding her that he'd helped her had probably been enough to manipulate her into agreeing to help him. Now Amy might be paying the price for that decision.

Paige pulled her jacket tighter around herself as they walked down the front path. It was windy today, and for the first time since last winter, the wind had an icy chill to it. It sliced through her red leather jacket and sent her curls whipping around her face, making her wish she'd taken the time to put her hair into a bun like she usually did. She'd gotten distracted making phone calls about Danielle's friend, then she'd taken Hayley for breakfast before dropping her off at school. It was important to her that as well as spending time together as a family, she and Elias each spent one-on-one time with the girls. She wanted Hayley and Arianna to know that both of their parents were always there for them and that they could tell them anything. She never wanted secrets to tear their family apart the way secrets had destroyed the Oliver family.

At the front door, Ryan knocked once.

They didn't expect an answer and got none.

Either Amy was Austin's next victim or the two of them had already split. They knew the two were working together. Sally Shield had positively identified Amy as the Amy she saw with Danielle, and DNA had Austin as Danielle's attacker. The two were partners, all they needed to find out was if they still were.

They already had an arrest warrant for both Amy and Austin, so when neither of them answered the door, Paige opened it.

The inside of the house was minimally furnished, with so much white it hurt her eyes. The walls and ceiling were painted white. The floor was polished concrete in a very light gray, and other than a couple of statement pieces in vivid red, blue or green, every piece of furniture and the entire kitchen was white. Paige felt like she'd walked inside a snowflake.

"Two sets of dishes in the sink, and a man's pair of shoes over in the corner there." Ryan pointed to the far corner of the room.

The downstairs of the house was basically one huge room, and it was clear that there was no one in here. That left the upstairs, and whatever rooms were behind the three doors down here.

Together—guns in hand—they made their way to the closest door. With Ryan covering her, Paige reached out a hand and quickly opened the door.

The bathroom was empty.

They moved on to the next room. It was a study with a desk filled with a computer and dozens of papers and bookcases crammed with books on interior design. It was similarly empty.

That only left one more room down here, and Paige was beginning to feel like Austin and Amy weren't here. In her mind, she was already trying to figure out where Austin might flee.

The last door led to the garage, which had bare walls and a car.

Paige looked at Ryan, and he nodded.

A car meant that Austin could still be here.

Carefully, the two of them made their way upstairs, they didn't want a repeat of what had happened at Ian Brownlee's house. While their job could be dangerous, most criminals didn't behave like Ian had. Most accepted their fate. But would Austin? Paige had the feeling that he would not. That he was going to come at them swinging when they found him.

Upstairs there were four bedrooms with en suites. From the clothes scattered all over the floor and the furniture, one clearly belonged to Amy. Two were obviously spare bedrooms, but the fourth had a closet full of Austin's clothes. It looked like he wasn't just hiding out here but that he lived here with his sister. Maybe the staying at friends' houses was just to make sure no one figured out how close he was with his sister.

Unfortunately, there were no signs of Austin himself.

"He's not here," Ryan said.

"But he was, and he might not be far away. The car was still here," she reminded him. "Maybe he's out jogging or something."

"Maybe," Ryan agreed but didn't sound like he really believed it. "Or he just stole or hired another car and is long gone. We should go through everything that's here and see if we can figure out where he might be."

"We should call in backup to help," she suggested. They really needed to find Austin as soon as possible. Just because he had engineered Danielle's abduction to frame his father didn't mean he wouldn't do it again. And there was still the question of whether Amy was still a willing participant in his game.

"May as well. It'll make things go quicker."

"Jack said if he and Xavier were done with their case they'd be happy to help." Jack was an ex-boyfriend of hers and Ryan's older brother, and Xavier was Annabelle's husband and a good friend of both of theirs. Both were amazing cops as well as great friends, and Paige knew that if the four of them put their heads together, then they'd be able to figure out where Austin was and what his next move was.

"Okay," Ryan agreed.

"I'll go start searching the study and call them," she said. Leaving Ryan to begin searching Austin's room, Paige headed back downstairs. There was no attic and no basement, so they had cleared the house, but something felt off.

A feeling in her gut that said they weren't alone.

Was there a secret room here, something like the one in the Oliver house?

It would make sense if Austin intended to turn on his sister all along. And the house had been recently built, for all they knew, maybe Austin had the place built then put it in his sister's name.

There were no carpets or rugs here so there couldn't be a secret trapdoor hidden underneath. If she were Austin, where would she put a hidden room?

Her eyes scanned the room, searching for anything that stood out.

What would Austin do?

He needed something that wouldn't be immediately noticeable and yet had easy access.

Her gaze stopped at the kitchen.

The pantry, maybe?

She hurried to it and stepped inside. It was large and big enough for four or five people to stand in comfortably. The shelves were mostly bare, and now that she was looking for it, they didn't quite meet up on one side.

Paige felt about on the shelves, and a moment later, one sprang backward.

Behind it was a narrow staircase. With her gun in hand, Paige slowly made her way down it. Austin and Amy could be in there, and she had no idea of what condition Amy would be in. Now that the door was open, she couldn't call out to Ryan because if they were there, they might hear her, and she might have already alerted them to her presence by opening the door, so she couldn't go and get Ryan either. For the moment, she was on her own.

At the bottom of the steps, there was an equally narrow hallway. Paige wondered if Austin had this house specially built with his games in mind. The man seemed to like to be prepared, and he was a planner and a manipulator.

The hallways twisted and turned for several yards before it finally opened into a small, dark room, maybe ten feet by ten feet.

Inside the room was Amy Murphy.

She was lying naked on a table, her wrists and ankles were cuffed with leather straps to the corners of the table. She had a tube down her nose and what looked like a catheter, and just like Danielle Terry, her mouth and eyes had been sewn closed.

Although she couldn't see, Amy's head was tilted toward the door, and the expression on her face was one that implied she knew someone was here but also that it wasn't her brother.

"Mmhmm," she mumbled through her closed lips.

"It's okay, Amy," she said as she hurried toward the young woman. "I'm a police officer."

She expected the woman to calm down at her words, but Amy only grew more agitated. Amy kept gesturing her head in the direction of the door, and Paige realized what she was trying to say.

Someone was coming.

Austin.

* * * * *

1:21 P.M.

If he hadn't had the secret hiding space in his closet, they would have caught him.

Not for the first time, Austin was exceedingly glad he had had this house built. It had been a stroke of genius. At the time, he hadn't known exactly why he was going to need a house with secret rooms including the room in the basement, which was where he was headed right now.

Austin adjusted the cop on his shoulders into a more comfortable position. He'd knocked the man out, so he was a dead weight, and he wanted to get him someplace safe. Cops usually came in pairs, like the Bananas in Pajamas, and he wanted to stash this man and go hunting for his partner who had to be around here somewhere.

He noticed her too late.

"Put him down and put your hands on your head," a voice ordered. He recognized the voice. These were the same cops who had interviewed him about the fire at his biological father's house. Detective Hood and Detective Xander. The woman was pretty. She might make a good addition to his collection; he might keep her around for a while and play with her.

Now, though, he had to decide his next move.

He only had seconds because he knew without a shadow of a doubt this woman wouldn't hesitate to do whatever was necessary to protect herself, her partner, and Amy.

"Don't do anything stupid, Austin," she told him.

He wouldn't.

134

Only their definition of stupid might differ.

He wouldn't do anything that he considered to be stupid. He would do whatever it took to walk out of here alive.

"We can get you help, Austin. You're sick, but we can get you help."

A doctor had told him that once.

That he was sick.

He had fantasized for months about ripping out every single one of her fingernails and toenails and relishing every single scream.

He had never gotten a chance to do it. He'd been ten, and abducting a respected therapist and finding someplace to keep her where he could enact his fantasies had been out of the question.

It wasn't now.

Maybe he'd see if that was as fun as he had imagined.

"I'm not going to ask you again, Austin. Put my partner down, get down on your knees, and put your hands behind your head."

Her voice was set.

She'd made up her mind.

Austin estimated that she was going to give him maybe another twenty or thirty seconds and then she was going to shoot him.

That she didn't have a gun pointed at him never even entered his mind.

But she wasn't the only one who was armed.

He counted to five, then dropped the cop from his shoulders, and spun around in one fluid movement.

The cop hesitated.

He didn't.

That was the difference of who was going to come out on top.

Austin fired off a shot milliseconds before the detective and hit her in the hand that was holding the gun, causing her weapon to clatter uselessly to the floor. The shot that she had fired went wide and plowed into the wall beside him.

He had to give it to her. Detective Hood didn't let a bullet through her hand slow her down. She launched at him, but the odds were stacked firmly against her. She was physically smaller and weaker than him, and she'd been shot.

She kept her body low and tried to knock him off his feet, but he wrapped an arm around her and yanked her up against his body. That didn't stop her from frantically trying to dislodge herself from his grip.

The struggle might have been fun, but he really didn't have time for it. He now had two cops he had to get restrained before something had a chance to go wrong.

He wasn't going to prison.

He'd rather die.

Part of him had always known he was going to die young. It was like he had lived his entire life with a death wish, only he'd been too afraid to actually pull the trigger. It wasn't like he wanted these cops to kill him, but he also didn't really care if they did.

Most people didn't know what it was like to live completely prepared for death. Most people fought against death with every ounce of strength they possessed. They worked out religiously, they dieted, they had plastic surgery performed to try and con themselves into believing they were cheating the clock.

But life was really death dressed up in disguise.

From the moment you were born, you were walking steadily toward it.

He had just embraced that from an early age. The thrill of seeing what he could do to himself to get as close to death without metaphorically getting his fingers burned had consumed him, but now he'd grown tired of that. Now he wanted to see how close he could get another person to death without actually pushing them over. Now he had three test subjects. He just had to figure out what to do with them. If the cops were here, then they knew Amy was involved, and when these two didn't return, someone would come looking for them.

"It's only a matter of time, Austin," Detective Hood told him.

"You may as well give yourself up. You're not going to be able to hide down here forever."

She was probably right, but he figured he could at least hide for a little while. He'd get these two situated, check on Amy, then go and move their car, so it wasn't like a beacon drawing the other cops in.

Where should he put her?

He hadn't planned on storing several people down here.

Maybe he could attach her to one of the chains and the guy to the other—that could work for now, at least. He could always make more permanent arrangements later once he'd had a chance to think things over.

Dragging her wriggling form over to the chains, he quickly snapped it around the cop's good wrist, assuming she'd be less likely to do any damage with the one he'd shot. Then he attached the other cop to the other chain. The man was still out cold, which worked to his advantage.

"Why are you doing this, Austin? What do you want to achieve?" Detective Hood asked. "You're smart. You know this isn't going to last long. You know they're coming for you. Why are you making this harder on yourself? It didn't work. We know your father didn't do anything to Danielle. It was you. It was all you. We found your DNA under her fingernails."

So that was what had given him away.

Austin wished he'd had a little more time the day he'd left her there.

The whole thing had been such a big risk, if he hadn't had Maya to help him, then he'd never have been able to do it. Maya hadn't known about the girl in the basement, but having her in his life had meant he'd known when the family had taken a vacation, which had given him the time he'd needed to construct the small room under Mateo's study. It had been a calculated risk. He knew that they didn't use the basement other than that one corner where the washer and dryer were, but there was always the chance that one of them could stumble upon the room before he was ready.

That they would eventually find it was the whole point, but not until he had the girl inside. He wanted them to find it and believe that it was Mateo who'd put her there. He wanted to turn them against his father. Mateo hadn't wanted him, yet he had gone and built another family—one that had no place for him. It seemed only fitting that his family should turn their backs on Mateo, just as he had done to Austin.

"And what you did to your sister," the detective continued, "it's not worth it. It's really not. Please, Austin, it's not too late. Turn yourself in, and you might be able to make a deal. You could go to a psychiatric hospital and get better. It's not too late."

He really had to shut her up.

She was making him angry, and bad things happened when he got angry.

"You don't get it," he said as he collected a needle and thread; he really was glad that he'd taken the time to learn the medical procedures he needed for this.

"Then explain it to me."

He looked at her. She appeared to be sincere. He'd never had anyone sincerely interested in wanting to understand him. His mother had just wanted him to be normal, to be like all the other kids. His biological father had wanted to pretend that he didn't exist. His adopted father wanted to control him, make him behave the way he thought he should. His sister was the good child of the family, but he had her so brainwashed that she didn't know what to think when it came to him. He had friends, but they were just people he used for his own purposes. They didn't really even know him well enough to care about him one way or the other.

But if this cop truly wanted to understand, then he'd tell her.

"You only know you're alive when you come close enough to death to taste it," he told her.

The detective shook her head. "You know you're alive when

you feel the breeze brush across your skin or you see a flock of birds moving in unison, or your baby laughs one of those great big belly laughs of pure joy."

That was the most ludicrous answer he'd ever heard. He could tell she was sincere by the look on her face, but that was because she had never stared death in the face before. She didn't know what it felt like, what it looked like, what it smelled like.

Soon, she would.

Soon, she would learn what he had many years ago. She'd know the rush of beating death, of taunting it, of letting it think that it had you only to snatch yourself away.

Death always won, but it didn't mean that you didn't have to make it work for it.

To him, death had always been more like a living breathing entity than just a state of being.

Yes, he realized the irony of likening death to a living being.

Death was his friend, and he enjoyed their rivalry, just like he was going to enjoy introducing him to his sister and the detectives.

* * * * *

1:53 P.M.

She was never going to be able to talk her way out of this.

Austin was on a whole other planet.

Paige could tell by looking into his eyes that he was serious about his death theory. Maybe that's why he had been obsessed with hurting himself as a child; maybe he'd wanted to get as close to death as he could without actually dying.

She had to figure out a way out of here.

People knew they were here, but it would be ages before anyone noticed they were gone. It wouldn't be until they didn't return home tonight that their spouses would notice something was wrong and report them missing.

By then, it would be too late.

Austin had a bobbin of coarse black thread and a needle in his hands.

She didn't have to have a very active imagination to figure out what he planned to do with them.

"Soon, you'll understand," he said, threading his needle.

"Understand what? Death?" If anyone understood death, she certainly did. "You're not the only one who's almost died, Austin."

Intrigued, he paused, studying her inquisitively. "You've almost died?"

"Yes. I had a stalker. He tried to beat me to death, and then he tried to drown me, then he came after me one last time while I was recovering in the hospital. I know what death feels like, it's cold—icy cold. And it looks like loneliness, there's no one there but you, and whether you live or die is up to you. If you want to live, then you have to fight for it. Doctors and family and friends can try to help, but in the end, it comes down to you. Do you want to live, Austin?"

The question seemed to catch him by surprise, and he cocked his head as he thought. "I'm ambivalent," he answered honestly. "I don't necessarily wish to be dead right this second, but if I were to die, I wouldn't mind. I'm not afraid of death. I think of him as a friend of sorts. I like that you've already met him, maybe I'll keep you around for a while."

He shot her what she thought he believed was a genuine smile, but instead, it was just creepy.

He meant what he'd just said.

Austin thought of death as a friend—one he wanted to share. He wanted to take his game of hovering as close to death as you could without actually touching it and bring others in on it.

With the threaded needle in his hands, he leaned toward her.

She had to do something to hold him off.

Ryan was hanging limply from the chain beside her, but she couldn't tell if he was still unconscious or if he was planning something.

Paige knew she had to make her move now. If she waited much longer, he was going to sew her mouth and her eyes closed. That was, of course, something she didn't want to experience. She just needed the briefest of distractions and then she might be able to grab the gun. He'd shoved his in the waistband of his jeans. If she could just get to it, then she wouldn't hesitate to shoot him.

"I died once," she told him.

"Oh?" His brown eyes lit up.

"When my stalker tried to drown me, he succeeded. I stopped breathing. I was dead. Thankfully, I was found in time and revived, but death isn't something fun, Austin. It's not a game. It's leaving behind the people you love and care about." If she didn't make it out of this room alive, then the thing that would hurt the most, more than any horrible thing Austin had planned for them, was knowing she was leaving behind the husband and daughters she adored.

"You're married?" He nodded at her left hand which hung from the metal cuff and chain.

"Yes."

"Kids?"

"Two little girls."

"See, that's the difference between us. You have something on earth holding you here. I don't. When you have nothing, you have nothing to leave."

In a way, that was true.

It was also what made Austin Rupert so dangerous.

He had nothing to live for except this. His games, torturing people, this was what made him happy, and he was completely at peace dying when it was over, whenever that would be.

With no further preamble, he grabbed at her, catching her face between his huge hands. She tried to fight against him, but he was too big, and she was badly balanced with one arm stretched above her head and having to perch on her toes because the chain was too high to allow her to stand properly.

Austin pinched his fingers between her cheeks and shoved the needle through her bottom lip. It hurt, but she'd experienced worse pain than that before. It was the fear of not being able to breathe or to see that was much more terrifying.

He was moving the needle toward her top lip when Amy suddenly launched off the table.

Before Austin walked into the room, Paige had been able to cut free one of the woman's wrists, then leave her with a knife to get the rest of the cuffs off.

Despite being unable to see, Amy seemed to be able to sense where things were and what was going on, as though her other senses had heightened. She had now shoved the knife into her brother's back, burying it deep in his flesh.

That was all the distraction she needed.

Paige lifted her injured hand—that she knew should hurt because he'd shot it, but now there was too much adrenalin flooding her system to feel pain—and grabbed for the gun.

Her hand was slick with blood, and it almost slipped through her fingers.

At the last second, she was able to grab hold of it.

Austin felt the gun leave his waistband and threw his sister across the room. Amy landed with a sickening thud and Austin spun around to face her, already reaching for the gun.

Aiming for his head, she fired.

He was out to kill her, anything less than shooting to kill wasn't going to work.

The bullet hit its target and Austin dropped.

For a moment, she couldn't quite believe it.

Paige felt like she was in a horror movie and at any second Austin was going to rise and come at them again.

"Are you all right?"

She heard her partner's words, but it was like she was hearing him from underwater.

"Paige?"

Ryan jostled her, and it nudged her out of the fog that was descending upon her.

"Are you okay? He shot you."

Now that it was over, and they were safe, the pain finally came. She wobbled a little, suddenly lightheaded.

Ryan wrapped an arm around her waist, helping to steady her.

"Are you okay?" she asked him. He'd been hurt, too, and up until a moment ago, possibly unconscious.

"I came around as he chained me up. I wanted him to think I was out while I tried to think up a plan. Seems like I didn't need to bother, you had things under control."

Yeah, right.

She'd been flying by the seat of her pants, and it was only by luck things had worked out.

The thread was hanging from her mouth, tugging uncomfortably, and she reached up to pull it out, but her injured hand was shaking so badly she couldn't get a grip on it.

"Leave it, Paige, the medics will pull it out when they get here."

Her partner was right.

She probably should do that.

But she couldn't.

She needed it out.

Having it there was a reminder of what Austin had been about to do, and it was triggering her claustrophobia.

Her blood pressure was already rising, her heart starting to race, her pulse starting to pound.

It needed to come out.

Now.

Right this second.

Ryan seemed to sense that because he balanced her against his body and released her. Taking hold of the needle, he pulled it until the thread came all the way out.

The metallic taste of blood trickled down her throat, but the relief she felt was overwhelming.

"Mmhmm." Amy was suddenly in front of them, thrusting something at them.

The key.

Somehow, she'd managed to locate the key without being able to see.

Ryan took it and unlocked his cuff, then hers, and lowered her to sit on the ground. He shrugged out of his sweater and wrapped it around her injured hand, then held her hand above her head to help slow the loss of blood. While her partner pulled out his phone and called for backup, Amy lay down beside them, her naked body shaking, and Paige hoped that she was all right.

She looked up at Ryan. "How's your head?"

"I'll live."

They'd come so close to dying.

If Amy hadn't been able to get free and distract Austin, then she'd have her mouth and eyes sewed shut by now.

But Amy *had* gotten free.

And she *had* gotten the gun.

Now they *would* live.

Offering her partner a half smile, she said, "We swapped this time. I got the gunshot wound, and you got the head wound."

Ryan chuckled. "Next time let's both try to walk away injury free."

Her partner keeping pressure on her wound was making it hurt worse, but in a way, it was a good kind of pain. It was the kind of pain that reminded you that you were alive, and nothing could beat that.

It had been a rough week. All she wanted was to go home and help her kids get dressed in their costumes and take them trick-or-treating. Their joy and excitement were just the balm her battered body and soul needed right now.

* * * * *

6:23 P.M.

"How do I look, Mommy?"

Hayley had insisted on getting herself dressed in her Halloween costume up in her room on her own. She'd said she wanted to surprise them. Her little girl was growing up, becoming so independent. Paige was so proud of her. She would miss being more needed in Hayley's life, but she also knew it would still be a long time before her daughter was completely self-sufficient.

Paige looked at the stairs as Hayley came down in her bear costume looking ridiculously adorable.

"You are the cutest, cuddliest bear there ever was," she exclaimed as Hayley giggled and came running over to hug her. Paige gave her daughter a one-armed hug. Her injured hand had been stitched and swathed in bandages, then her arm placed in a sling to help keep the hand immobilized as it healed. Ryan had also been treated and released. Amy had been admitted to the hospital. The stitches her brother had put in had been removed, and her doctors were hopeful she would recover.

"Look at Ari." Hayley clapped her hands and ran her fingers over the sequins they'd sewn over the words "Honey Pot" together.

"I think we're the best-looking family of bears," Elias declared.

When they'd settled on the bear and honey pot costumes for Hayley and Arianna, Hayley had asked her and Elias to dress as bears as well, saying that they were a family, so they should dress like one. Paige certainly couldn't argue with that logic. Although it had been a lot of work, she'd loved every second of working on sewing the costumes. She loved doing anything that related to her family.

"We are." Hayley giggled again.

She loved hearing her serious little girl laugh so much. Of all the first holidays they had celebrated as a family, Mother's Day and Father's Day had been her favorites because she'd started thinking that they would never get to be parents. This was quickly surpassing even the joy of those days.

Hayley was so happy, and if anyone deserved some happiness, it was Hayley. To go from being kept a prisoner in a house for the first five years of her life to where she was now was amazing. *Hayley* was amazing.

"Can we go now?" Hayley looked like she was bursting with excitement.

"We sure can," Elias said, setting the bowl of candy for the trick-or-treaters on a small table outside the front door.

As Paige stood, balancing Arianna on her hip, she took a moment just to look at her family. They looked ridiculous in their bear costumes—and awesome. They looked like a unit, which they were.

Nothing could ever tear them apart.

Problems may come and go, but her family would weather them together.

They loved one another, and corny as it was, it was true, love conquered all. It didn't make everything perfect or easy, but it sustained you through the times where things were imperfect and hard.

She had been silly. She'd been overthinking things and inventing troubles where there weren't any. She may be biased, but she had the best family in the entire world.

Who cared that her girls were adopted?

It didn't make her love them any less, and it wouldn't make them love her any less. A mother wasn't someone who carried a child in their womb. A mother was someone who was by your side when you were sick, when you laughed, and when you cried. They celebrated your achievements with you and commiserated over your failures. They loved you and would sacrifice anything for you.

Paige knew she couldn't have loved Hayley and Arianna more if they'd grown inside her, and she knew they loved her just as much as if they had.

Tomorrow at work there would be more cases, more people murdered or mutilated or assaulted, but tonight was about having fun with her family. Pulling on her bear hood, she passed Arianna to Elias, handed Hayley her purple pumpkin trick-or-treat bucket, then took her daughter's hand, and together the four of them walked out into the night to join the other happy families.

"How much candy can I get, Mommy?" Hayley asked.

"As much as you want."

About the Author

Jane has loved reading and writing since she can remember. She writes dark and disturbing crime/mystery/suspense with some romance thrown in because, well, who doesn't love romance?! She has several series including the complete Detective Parker Bell series, the Count to Ten series, the Christmas Romantic Suspense series, and the Flashes of Fate series of novelettes.

When she's not writing Jane loves to read, bake, go to the beach, ski, horse ride, and watch Disney movies. She has a black belt in Taekwondo, a 200+ collection of teddy bears, and her favorite color is pink. She has the world's two most sweet and pretty Dalmatians, Ivory and Pearl. Oh, and she also enjoys spending time with family and friends!

To connect and keep up to date please visit any of the following

Email – mailto:janeblytheauthor@gmail.com
Facebook – http://www.facebook.com/janeblytheauthor
Instagram – http://www.instagram.com/jane_blythe_author
Reader Group – http://www.facebook.com/groups/janeskillersweethearts
Twitter – http://www.twitter.com/jblytheauthor
Website – http://www.janeblythe.com.au

sic enim dilexit Deus mundum ut Filium suum unigenitum daret ut omnis qui credit in eum habeat vitam aeternam